"Why did you say you needed to talk to me?"

"Pull over."

This had to be bad news. "Why?"

He touched her arm, and she recoiled. She wanted nothing more to do with Mister Perfect. He was toying with her, asking inane questions and hinting at dire circumstances.

She yanked the steering wheel and made a hard right onto a side street. Halfway down the block, she parked and turned off the engine. Eve preferred facts to innuendo. She wanted the truth, no matter how horrible.

"All right, Blake, I'm parked. If you have something to tell me, get on with it."

His eyes flicked as if he was searching her face, trying to gauge her reaction. "It might be better if I gave you more information. Set the framework."

"Just spit it out." She braced herself. "Am I dying?"

He cleared his throat. "Eve, I have reason to believe that you're pregnant."

"That's impossible."

She was a virgin.

CASSIE MILES

LOCK, STOCK AND SECRET BABY

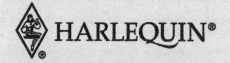

TORONTO • NEW YORK • LONDON
AMSTERDAM • PARIS • SYDNEY • HAMBURG
STOCKHOLM • ATHENS • TOKYO • MILAN • MADRID
PRAGUE • WARSAW • BUDAPEST • AUCKLAND

Recycling programs
for this product may
not exist in your area.

ISBN-13: 978-0-373-69490-7

LOCK, STOCK AND SECRET BABY

Copyright © 2010 by Kay Bergstrom

This is a work of fiction. Names, characters, places and incidents are
either the product of the author's imagination or are used fictitiously,
and any resemblance to actual persons, living or dead, business
establishments, events or locales is entirely coincidental.

This edition published by arrangement with Harlequin Books S.A.

For questions and comments about the quality of this book please contact
us at Customer_eCare@Harlequin.ca.

www.eHarlequin.com

Printed in U.S.A.

ABOUT THE AUTHOR

Though born in Chicago and raised in L.A., Cassie Miles has lived in Colorado long enough to be considered a semi-native. The first home she owned was a log cabin in the mountains overlooking Elk Creek, with a thirty-mile commute to her work at the *Denver Post*.

After raising two daughters and cooking tons of macaroni and cheese for her family, Cassie is trying to be more adventurous in her culinary efforts. Ceviche, anyone? She's discovered that almost anything tastes better with wine. When she's not plotting Harlequin Intrigue books, Cassie likes to hang out at the Denver Botanical Gardens near her high-rise home.

Books by Cassie Miles

**Rocky Mountain Safe House
†Safe House: Mesa Verde
*Christmas at the Carlisles'
††Special Delivery Babies

CAST OF CHARACTERS

Eve Weathers—A brilliant mathematician, she leaves her inner nerd behind in the struggle to protect her unborn baby.

Blake Jantzen—He returns from a Special Forces assignment to avenge his father's murder.

Dr. Ray Jantzen—Blake's father sacrificed everything to protect those he cared about.

Dr. Edgar Prentice—Partnered with Dr. Ray, he initiated a study of in vitro babies twenty-six years ago.

David Vargas—His financial genius is matched only by his intense ambition.

Dr. Trevor Lattimer—The doctor suffers from a debilitating infection that has left him nearly blind.

Peter Gregory, aka Pyro—His musical talent shines through in his explosive rock and roll.

General Stephen Walsh—An old friend of Blake's father, he provides the tools to help in the investigation.

Chapter One

Clutter spilled across the desktop in Ray Jantzen's home office: unopened junk mail, books, a running shoe with a broken lace, file folders, research notes for a paper he'd published in the *American Journal of Psychiatry* and...a gun.

Behind a stack of magazines, he located a framed photograph of his late wife, Annie, and their son, Blake. The sight of his beloved Annie's smile wrenched at his heart. She'd passed away two years ago, a month shy of their fortieth anniversary.

With his thumb, Ray wiped a smudge from the glass and focused on the image of his son. Though Blake was only eight in this picture, his dark brown eyes snapped with impatient intelligence. *Gifted* wasn't a sufficient word to describe him. And yet, he hadn't chosen a career where he could concentrate on his intellect. At age twenty-five, Blake was part of a Special Forces team working undercover in undisclosed locations.

Setting aside the photo, Ray opened his laptop and typed an e-mail.

My dear son, I loved you from the moment you emerged from your mother's womb with

a squall and two clenched fists. Forgive me for
what I'm about to disclose...

He was well aware of his pompous phrasing, clearly
a defense mechanism to hide his shame. He should have
told Blake long ago. After four decades as a psychiatrist,
Ray should have been wiser. Unspoken secrets never went
away. The lies one told festered beneath the surface and
arose in times of stress to bite one's ass.

His e-mail ended with: Take care of Eve Weathers.
She needs you.

He hit Send, closed the laptop and took it to the safe
hidden behind the bookshelves. Like the rest of his office,
the interior of the safe had accumulated a great deal of
paper. But these notes were precious; they would tell the
whole truth about the story he hinted at in his e-mail.

After locking the safe and closing the hinged section of
bookshelves, he went to the window. The red, yellow and
magenta tulips in his garden bobbed in the June breezes.
The sun was setting behind the foothills west of Denver.
So beautiful. He should have spent more time outdoors.

The door to his office opened. A melodic voice said,
"Good evening, Dr. Jantzen."

"How did you get inside?"

"Your alarm system is rudimentary. Your locks, pa-
thetic." The extraordinary tonal quality of the intruder's
voice hinted at his immense musical talent. "And this office
is a rat's nest. How do you work?"

"I like it this way."

"And what does that say about your emotional state?
Hmm? Disorganized thinking, perhaps?"

Angered by this mocking analysis, Ray turned away
from the window and faced the intruder. His eyes were
silver, like the barrel of his Beretta.

Ray lunged for his own weapon. It trembled in his hand. He'd never be able to shoot this young man whom he had known literally since birth.

"You're not a killer." The voice was sheer music. "Put down the gun."

Ray sank into the chair behind his desk and reached for the telephone. Still holding the gun, he hit the speed dial for the security service that monitored his "rudimentary" alarm system. They were guaranteed to respond within ten minutes.

"Hang up the phone, Dr. Jantzen."

"Or else?"

"Be reasonable." He aimed the Beretta. "You know what I'm looking for."

Turning over his records wouldn't be enough, and Ray knew it. "I won't remain silent. I can't."

"Then you will die."

Ray squeezed off several shots, aiming high. He hoped to frighten his opponent, though he knew that hope was futile.

Three bullets burned into his chest. Before his eyelids closed, he imprinted his gaze on the photograph of Blake and his beloved Annie.

EVE WEATHERS HAD ATTENDED many funerals, mostly in the company of her parents, mostly for people she didn't know. Being raised on army bases meant death visited her community with a sad and terrible frequency. But she'd never before stood at the graveside of someone who'd been murdered.

The bright sun of an early June afternoon dimmed, as if a shadow hung over them, as if they all shared in the guilt. The police said Dr. Ray Jantzen had been killed by a burglar. They had no suspects. The killer might even be among them.

While the preacher read from Psalms, she checked out the other graveside mourners. Her mother would have called this a good turnout—close to a hundred people. An eclectic bunch, they appeared to be from all walks of life. There were serious-looking older men who were probably Ray's friends and psychiatrist coworkers, several men in uniform because Ray had worked at the VA hospital, a young man in leather with spiky, black hair and mirrored sunglasses, a couple of teenagers and various family members. Their only common denominator was that Eve didn't know any of them.

Dr. Ray had been in her life for as long as she could remember, literally since she was born. When her parents had applied for an experimental in vitro fertilization program at the army base where her dad had been stationed, Eve had become part of a lifelong study. Every year, she had filled in a questionnaire and had given Dr. Ray an update on her life, both her physical and emotional condition.

They'd only met in person a couple of times before she had moved to Boulder three years ago to take a mathematical engineering position at Sun Wave Labs. For the past two years, she and Dr. Ray had done their updates over dinner. His wife had passed away, and she assumed he was lonely.

The sound of his coffin being lowered startled her. She blinked. Her gaze lit upon a dark-haired man in a black suit who stood beside the preacher. She recognized him from the photo Dr. Ray had carried in his wallet. His son, Blake Jantzen.

She studied Blake with a mathematician's eye, taking his measure. His physical proportions were remarkable. Her mind calculated the inches and angles of his shoulders, his torso and the length of his legs. Though he wasn't splayed out, like Da Vinci's *Vitruvian Man,* Blake Jantzen was close to ideal.

When his gaze met hers, a tremor rippled through her, and she immediately lowered her eyes. She hadn't meant to stare, hadn't intended to intrude on what had to be a terrible day for him. When she looked up again, he was still watching her.

Their eye contact intensified. His dark eyes bored into hers, and that little tremor expanded to a full-blown, pulsating earthquake inside her rib cage. If she didn't look away, it felt as if her heart would explode. This wasn't how she usually reacted to men, even if they were practically perfect.

Pretending to pray, she stared down at her feet. Her toes protruded from her hiking sandals which were really too casual for a funeral, even if they were black. Suddenly self-conscious, she decided her black skirt was too short, showing off way too much of her winter white legs. She buttoned her black cotton jacket over her white tank top, stained with a dribble of coffee from this morning.

Whenever she mingled with the general public, her style seemed inadequate. In the lab, she wore comfortable jeans and T-shirts with nerdy slogans. Her chin-length, wheat-blond hair resembled a bird's nest. None of the guys she worked with cared what she looked like. They were so absorbed in their work that they wouldn't notice if she showed up naked, except perhaps to comment on the small tattooed symbol for pi above her left breast.

The crowd dispersed, and she lost sight of Blake, which was probably for the best. Her mother would have told her that the proper behavior would be to shake his hand and offer condolences, but she didn't trust herself to get that close to him without a meltdown. Was she so desperate for male companionship that she'd hit on a guy at his father's funeral?

She made a beeline for her car. As she clicked the door lock, she heard a voice behind her. "Are you Eve Weathers?"

Without turning around, she knew who that sexy baritone belonged to. "I'm Eve."

"I'm Blake Jantzen. I need to talk to you."

Up close, he was even more amazing. Was there a degree beyond perfection? Most people had incongruities in their facial structure: one eye higher than the other, a bump on the nose or a dimple in one cheek and not the other. Blake had none of those anomalies. Even the shadows of exhaustion beneath his eyes were precisely symmetrical.

She stammered, "I'm s-sorry for your loss."

He acknowledged with a crisp nod. "Come back to the house. My aunt arranged a reception."

"I don't know where you live."

"My father's house," he clarified.

Though she'd planned to return to her office in Boulder, she couldn't refuse without being rude. "I've never been to Dr. Ray's home."

A flicker of surprise registered in his coffee-brown eyes. "I thought you were close to him. He thought highly of you."

"We met for dinner a couple of times, and he was very kind to me. But it was always at a restaurant. He kept his private life, well, private." Her parents never could have afforded her postgrad studies if Dr. Ray hadn't helped her obtain scholarships. "I thought of him as a benefactor."

"Stay here," Blake said. "I'll tell my aunt that I'm riding with you."

Though she obediently slid behind the steering wheel of her hybrid and waited, his attitude irked her. Blake had the arrogant tone of someone who gave orders that must be followed. *A military guy.* An alpha male. The kind of man who demanded too much and gave little in return. If she ever fell in love, she hoped it would be with a guy who at least pretended to treat her as an equal.

Though she doubted that she and Blake would get along, Eve checked her reflection in the visor mirror. She'd shed a couple of tears, but the mascara around her blue eyes wasn't smudged. She pushed her bangs into a semblance of order.

In a matter of minutes, Mr. Perfect returned to her car and climbed into the passenger side. "At the exit from the cemetery, turn right."

Having issued his order, he leaned back in the seat and closed his eyes.

Eve wished there was something she could do or say to comfort him. Her mother was good in these situations; she knew how to show empathy without being too sentimental. Eve lacked those people skills. She could calculate quadratic equations in the blink of an eye, but the art of conversation baffled her. She pinched her lips and remained silent as she drove.

When Blake opened his eyes and leaned forward, he appeared to be completely in control. "What's your birthday?"

An odd question. "June twenty-second. I'll be twenty-six."

"Mine is June thirtieth. Same year," he said. "And you were born in New Mexico."

"At an army base near Roswell."

"Me, too."

"I guess we have something in common."

"More than you know," he said. "Tell me about your relationship with my dad."

Apparently, Mr. Perfect wasn't big on idle chatter. This felt like an interrogation. "I communicated with Dr. Ray once a year, every year. On my birthday, I filled out a status report with forty questions. Some of them were essay questions and took a while to answer."

"Did you ever wonder why?"

"Of course, I did." His terse questions provoked an equally abrupt response from her. "I'm not a mindless idiot."

He gave a short laugh. "I'd bet on the opposite. You're pretty damn smart."

"Maybe."

"Tell me what you know about my dad's status reports."

What was he getting at? He must already know this information. "Your father told me I was part of a study group made up of children with similar backgrounds and key genetic markers. He monitored potential and achievement, which was why he helped me get scholarships."

"Take a right at the next light."

She could feel his scrutiny as he studied her. Though she wasn't sure that she even liked this guy, she responded to him with an unwanted excitement that set her heart racing. Her brain fumbled for something to break the silence. "There was a good turnout for the funeral."

"Did you recognize anybody?"

"Not a soul. I kind of expected to see Dr. Prentice."

"How do you know Prentice?"

"He was the other half of the study your father worked on," she said. "As I'm sure you already know."

"Tell me, anyway."

"Your dad correlated the psychiatric data. And Prentice did medical examinations every few years or so. He contacted me about six weeks ago."

"The date?"

She pulled up her mental calendar. "It was April six-teenth, the day after tax day. Prentice said he needed to see me right away. There was an issue about possible exposure to radiation when I was a child."

"And you were scared."

"Terrified." There had been a similar scare five years ago that Dr. Prentice treated with a brief course of media-tion. "Radiation poisoning isn't something to mess around with. Turns out that I'm fine. Prentice gave me a clean bill of health."

"What do you remember about the testing?"

"It was a thorough physical." She wasn't about to go into details about the pelvic exam or the part where she'd been under anesthetic. "I went to a clinic after work on a Friday, and I didn't get home until after ten o'clock. Dr. Prentice's assistant drove me and made sure I got into bed."

"Any ill effects?"

Come to think of it she hadn't been feeling like her-self lately. Her stomach had been queasy. A couple of times, she'd vomited. "Do you know anything about the testing?"

"Yes," he said curtly.

Her fear returned with a vengeance. What did Blake know? Had he pulled her aside because he had bad news? She might have been poisoned by a childhood exposure, might have some awful disease. Her cells could be turning against her at this very moment. "Why did you say that you needed to talk to me?"

"Pull over."

This had to be bad news. "Why?"

He touched her arm, and she recoiled as if he'd poked her with a cattle prod. She wanted nothing more to do with

Mr. Perfect. He was toying with her, asking inane questions and hinting at dire circumstances.

She yanked the steering wheel and made a hard right onto a side street with wood-frame houses, skimpy trees and sidewalks that blended into the curb. Halfway down the block, she parked and turned off the engine. Eve preferred facts to innuendo. She wanted the truth, no matter how horrible.

"All right, Blake, I'm parked. If you have something to tell me, get on with it."

His eyes flicked as if he was searching her face, trying to gauge her reaction. "It might be better if I gave you more information. Set the framework."

"Just spit it out." She braced herself. "Am I dying?"

He cleared his throat. "Eve, I have reason to believe that you're pregnant."

"That's impossible."

She was a virgin.

Chapter Two

Blake watched her reaction, looking for a sign that Eve Weathers had been complicit in Prentice's scheme. He saw nothing of the kind.

His information had shocked her. She gasped, loudly and repeatedly. Her eyes opened wide. Pupils dilated. She was on the verge of hyperventilation. Her chest heaved against the seat belt. "I can't be pregnant."

"I said it was a possibility."

"Why would you say such a thing? And how the hell would you know?"

"Before he was murdered, my father sent me an e-mail." At the moment the e-mail was sent, Blake had been in a debriefing meeting at the Pentagon. He didn't read the message until two hours later. By then, it was too late. His father was dead.

"What did it say?"

Too much for him to explain right now. Blake cut to the pertinent facts. "My father received information that Dr. Prentice had implanted you with an embryo."

"During the examination? While I was unconscious?" She dragged her fingers through her pale blond hair. "That's sickening. Disgusting."

When she grasped the key in the ignition, he stayed her hand. Gently, he said, "Maybe you should let me drive."

She yanked away from him. "My car. I drive."

"You don't look so good," he said.

"Thanks so much."

"Not an insult." He liked her looks. "I meant that you appear to be in shock. I don't want you to pass out."

"Oh, I'm way too angry to faint." She started the car. "You want out?"

"No." He couldn't let her drive off by herself. In his e-mail, Dad had told Blake to take care of Eve Weathers. That last request could not be ignored.

She punched the accelerator and squealed away from the curb. Halfway down the street, she whipped a U-turn, barely missing a van parked at the curb.

His right foot pushed down on an invisible brake on the passenger-side floorboard. "If you let me drive, we can be at my father's house in ten minutes."

"That's not where we're going."

At the corner, she made an aggressive merge into traffic. Her tension showed in her white-knuckle grip on the steering wheel, but she wasn't reckless. She checked her mirrors before changing lanes and stayed within the speed limit. With a sudden swerve, she drove into the parking lot outside a convenience store.

Without a word, she threw off her seat belt and left the car. He trailed behind her. Inside the store, he asked, "You mind telling me what we're doing here?"

"Maybe I wanted a donut."

Her sarcasm was preferable to the moment of shock when he'd mentioned pregnancy. He should have been more careful, should have expected her reaction, but he wasn't operating at peak efficiency. Eve's problems weren't his primary concern.

His focus was on his father's murder. The cops were satisfied with the lame explanation that a burglar did the crime. *Like hell.* This killing wasn't a random act of violence. Blake was determined to find the son of a bitch who pulled the trigger and the men who sent him.

He stood behind Eve as she stared at shelves packed with an array of over-the-counter medicines. When she spied the pregnancy tests, she grabbed three of them. "Damn, I left my purse in the car."

"I'll pay," he said.

At the counter, the clerk gave them a knowing smirk as he rang up the purchase.

Eve added a pack of gum. "And two jerky sticks and one of these pecan things."

"There's food at the house," he said.

"I have a craving. Isn't that what pregnant women do?"

When she plucked a magazine off the rack below the counter, she set down her car keys. He snatched them. "I'm driving. It's easier than giving you directions."

"Fine," she growled. "You drive."

Back in the car, he adjusted the driver's seat for his long legs and headed toward his father's house while Eve tore open the packaging on the pregnancy tests and read the instructions. "When we get to the house," she said, "I'd appreciate being shown to the nearest bathroom."

He nodded.

"I won't make a scene," she assured him. "I respect your father's memory."

Several other vehicles were already parked on the street outside the long ranch-style house that his mother had loved so much. When they had first moved here fifteen years ago, there had been few other houses in the area. Development had crept closer, but his father's house still commanded an outstanding view. To the south, Pikes Peak was visible on a clear day like today.

No matter where in the world he was stationed, he treasured the memory of home—of translucent, Colorado skies and distant, snowcapped peaks. This vision was his solace and the basis for his daily meditation.

As they went up the sidewalk to the house, he pocketed her keys, not wanting her to have easy access to an escape until she calmed down.

Inside, he skirted the living room where people had gathered and escorted her down a long hallway that bisected the left half of the house. At the end of the hall, he opened the door to his dad's office. Unlike the rest of this well-maintained residence, this room looked like the aftermath of a tornado. In addition to the papers and magazines, a fine coating of fingerprint dust from the police investigation covered many of the surfaces. The supposedly secret safe in the bookshelves hung open in its hinges. His father's blood stained the Persian carpet behind the desk.

When he closed the door, Eve stood very still. "Is this where it happened?"

"Yes."

"You haven't cleaned up."

"Not yet." Valuable information could be hidden somewhere in this room. He'd already searched, but he would search again and again and again, until he found the killer.

IN THE PRIVACY OF THE bathroom, Eve almost yielded to the overwhelming pressure of anger and fear. If ever there had been a time in her life when she wanted to curl up in a ball and cry, this was it. She didn't want to be pregnant. Not now, possibly not ever. Having a baby wasn't on her agenda.

She knew that she'd skipped her last period but hadn't worried because Dr. Prentice told her she might be irregular after her testing. Prentice, that bastard. Why had she believed him? With good reason, damn it. She had twenty-five years of good faith; Prentice and Dr. Ray had been part of her life since birth.

Setting her purse on the counter, she took out the kits from the convenience store: three different brands. Two of the kits had two tests inside the box, and she set the extras aside.

She followed the simple instructions and arrayed the three test sticks on the counter beside the sink. Then, she waited, counting the seconds.

Each test had a different indicator. One showed a plus sign in the window to indicate a positive. Another showed a pink line. The third would turn blue.

Though counting didn't make time go faster, reciting numerical progressions had always soothed her. As a child, she learned to count prime numbers all the way up to 3,571—the first five hundred primes. Five hundred unique numbers, divisible only by themselves and one.

The last time she had seen Dr. Ray over dinner, she'd talked about prime. He had suggested—in his kindly way—that she might want to pursue deeper interpersonal relationships. Make friends, join groups, go on dates, blah, blah, blah.

She had told him that she was happy just as she was. Some people needed others to make them complete, but she was unique. Like a prime number, she was divisible only by herself. Singular.

If she was pregnant, she'd never be alone again.

One of the tests required only one minute to show results. She could look down right now and see. But the others needed five minutes, and she didn't want to peek until all the results were in and could be verified against each other.

But she couldn't wait. She looked down. The first test showed a positive.

Could she trust a kit from a convenience store? It hardly seemed scientific in spite of the claim on the box of ninety-nine percent accuracy in detecting a pregnancy hormone, hCG, released into the body by the placenta.

The second test repeated the positive. And the third.

She was pregnant, pregnant and pregnant.

Tentatively, she touched her lower abdomen. *Hello, in there. Can you hear me?* An absurd question. At this point in development, the fetus wouldn't have ears. But they shared the same body, the same blood. The food she ate nurtured the tiny being that grew within her. The miracle of life. Amazing. Infuriating.

Damn it, this couldn't be happening! She dug into her purse and found her cell phone. Dr. Prentice's private cell phone number was in the memory.

He answered after the fourth ring. "I've been expecting to hear from you, Eve."

"How could you do this to me?"

"I assume you're aware of—"

"I'm aware, damn you. I just took a pregnancy test."

"You're upset."

A mild description of her outrage. "You might as well have raped me."

"Not at all the same thing. Rape is an act of violence. You received the highest quality medical care. My intentions were for your own good. I could have hired a surrogate, you know."

"A what?"

"A surrogate mother. Some women rent out their wombs like cheap motels."

"I know what a surrogate is."

Her voice was louder than she intended. Blake knocked on the bathroom door. "Eve? Are you all right?"

She didn't want to deal with him. This wasn't his problem. Lowering her voice, she demanded, "Why, Dr. Prentice? Why would you do this?"

"Ray's research indicated the optimum condition for development comes when the biological mother carries the fetus and bonds with the infant."

Biological mother? Bonding? None of what he'd just said made sense. "I ought to hire a lawyer and sue you."

"Don't bother. When you came for your examination, you signed a consent form."

With a jolt, she remembered being handed several documents on a clipboard. "You told me it was a routine medical procedure."

"If you like, I can fax you a copy."

He knew her too well, knew that she wouldn't bother to read the fine print. She had trusted him. "I have to know why."

"To create the second generation."

"Second generation of what?"

From outside the bathroom door, she heard Blake. "Who are you talking to, Eve?"

"I'm fine," she told him.

"Unlock the damn door," Blake said.

"In a minute."

She moved to the farthest wall of the bathroom beside the toilet. A magazine stand held back issues of *Psychology Today*. Guest towels with a teal-blue border hung from a pewter rack. She spoke into the phone. "Signed consent form or not, this was wrong."

"What's done is done," he said.

"I'm not ready to be a mother." Everything in her life would have to change. She'd have to find a way to juggle work and child care. There was so much to learn, an over-whelming amount of research. How could she manage? "Maybe I should give the baby up for adoption."

"That would be a mistake."

"It's not your call, Dr. Prentice."

"Let me give you something else to consider. Do you re-member five years ago when I had you on medication?"

The earlier scare about possible radiation poisoning. "Another lie?"

"I'm a scientist," he said archly. "I don't deal in ethics. Five years ago, the medication I gave you was actually a fertility drug that encouraged ovulation. You produced several eggs which I then harvested during your physical exam. I used those eggs to create embryos."

"My egg?" The impact of this new information hit her hard. "You implanted me with my own egg?"

"The fetus you're carrying is biologically your own."

My baby. Her hand rested protectively on her stomach. She felt a deep, immediate connection. *This is my baby.*

"This entire process would have been far less compli-cated," Dr. Prentice said, "if Ray had agreed to facilitate. He had a decent grasp on your psychological development and could have convinced you that having this baby was a good idea. Brilliant, in fact. You're lucky to take part in—"

The room started to spin. Eve never fainted. But her knees went weak. *I'm having a baby.* She collapsed with a thud. The phone fell from her limp hand onto the tiled bathroom floor.

Chapter Three

Eve heard the sharp rap of knuckles against the bathroom door—a faraway sound, like pebbles being tossed down a well.

Blake called through the door, "Are you all right? Eve, answer me."

She wasn't all right. Too many variables swirled inside her head. Nothing made logical sense.

"I'm coming in," Blake said.

The doorknob turned. Through a haze, she saw him come closer. He knelt beside her. His fingers rested on her throat, checking her pulse.

"Locked door," she said. "How did you…"

"Picked the lock," he said. "Can you sit up?"

"I'm fine."

But she wasn't fine. Her eyelids closed, shutting out the light and the intolerable confusion. Her mind careened wildly. How could she be pregnant when she'd never made love? She had the result without the experience. People told her sex was great, but she hadn't tested the theory, didn't know for sure. There was a lot she didn't know, like how to be a mother. Would the baby look like her? A girl baby or a boy? Oh, God, what would she tell her parents?

She was aware of being lifted from the bathroom floor and carried like a little girl. If only she could go back to those more innocent times. Her childhood memories were happy. Not idyllic, but happy. Her parents had loved her, even though she had never quite fit in. She always felt different, like an alien girl who had beamed into their normal world from the planet Nerd.

When she opened her eyes, she was stretched out on the leather sofa in Dr. Ray's office with her feet elevated on a pillow. A crocheted green-and-yellow afghan covered her. Blake pressed a cool washcloth against her forehead.

"I'm going to have a baby," she whispered.

"I know." His smile reached his eyes, deepening the faint, symmetrical lines that radiated from the corners. Though he had no reason to care about her, he seemed concerned. Maybe Mr. Perfect had a heart, after all.

Her hand lingered on her flat stomach. An intuitive urge to protect the baby? She couldn't count on motherly instincts to show her the way. There were books to be read. More information was vital. She'd need a regimen of special vitamins and exercises. "I should go."

"You'll stay here tonight. I have an extra bedroom."

"Is that an order?"

He arched one eyebrow, disrupting the precise balance of his features. "That isn't what I meant."

"I know." She also knew that he couldn't stop himself from being bossy. With an effort, she swung her legs down to the floor and sat up on the sofa. The washcloth fell from her forehead. She wasn't dizzy, but an edge of darkness pressed against her peripheral vision.

He placed a bottle of water into her hand. "Drink."

No objection from her. Rehydrating her body was a very good idea. Tipping the bottle against her lips, she took a couple of sips. The cool liquid tasted amazing. A few drops slid down her chin, and she wiped them away.

Though she didn't feel capable of running a mile, her strength was returning. Arching her neck, she stretched.

"Does anything hurt?" Blake asked.

"Only my pride," she said. "I've never keeled over like that before."

"There's a first time for everything."

"Like being pregnant." Each and every thought circled back to that inevitable theme.

"Who were you talking to on the phone?" he asked.

"Dr. Prentice. That old toad." She still couldn't believe what he'd done to her. "You were right about him implanting an embryo, but here's the kicker. He used one of my own eggs. Biologically, I'm the mother of this baby."

"How did you reach Prentice?"

She shrugged. "I have his cell number."

"I need to talk to him. ASAP." His momentary compassion faded quickly. His jaw was so tense that his lips didn't move when he talked. "I want you to arrange a meeting with Prentice."

"After what he did to me? No way. I'm not getting within a hundred yards of Dr. Edgar Prentice."

"I don't expect you to come along. Set a meeting for me. A face-to-face meeting."

"What's going on?" She took another sip of water. "Is there some other horrible secret you haven't told me yet?"

Instead of responding, he rose to his feet. "You're feeling better. You should eat something."

His quick change of subject worried her. Eve wasn't usually good at reading other people's expressions, but she had a weird connection with Blake. She could tell that he was holding back. "If there's something else, I want to know."

He headed toward the door. "I'll bring a sandwich from the buffet table."

Before she could stop him, he left the office. Moving fast, he almost seemed to be fleeing from her, abandoning her. So much for counting on Blake for support.

Slowly, she rose from the sofa. Her legs steadied as she walked to the bathroom. On the countertop, the three pregnancy test sticks lined up to mock her. She shoved them into the trash and washed her hands. After splashing cold water on her face, she felt more alert, more aware and more certain that Blake was hiding something. What else could be wrong? Was this something to do with the father of her baby? She hadn't even considered that huge question. Prentice had chosen someone as a sperm donor. But who? *Oh, God, do I even want to know?*

She couldn't take much more. Finding out that she was pregnant had been devastating enough. She'd shattered like protons in a super collider. Could she take another life-changing jolt?

There was no other choice. *I need to know everything.* It was time to pull herself together. She picked up her cell phone and tucked it into her purse. She needed answers.

When she returned to the sofa, Blake slipped back into the office with a plate of fruit and a ham sandwich. The sight of food momentarily eclipsed her other concerns. She wolfed down half the sandwich in huge bites. Not the most ladylike behavior but she needed her strength.

"Eating for two?" he asked.

"Apparently so." She swallowed. "I should thank you for helping me when I fainted. You're good at taking care of people."

"I have paramedic training."

The way he'd treated her—elevating her feet, covering her with a blanket and giving her water—was standard procedure for shock. "Your dad mentioned that you're in the military."

"Correct."

"I was an army brat, so I know all about you guys. Let me guess. You're in Special Forces."

"Good guess."

"You're one of those scary dudes who can take out ten armed terrorists with a spoon and a paper clip."

He shrugged. "Not ten. Maybe six."

"I appreciate your ferociousness. I really do. But what I need from you right now doesn't involve physical mayhem. I want answers. There's something you're holding back, something else you haven't told me."

His reluctance showed when he paced away from her and went to the window—putting physical distance between them. "I'm not sure you can handle the truth."

"You're not saying that right. In the movie, it was like this." She made a fist and did a bad Jack Nicholson impression. "You can't handle the truth."

"I loved when he did that."

"Me, too." Laughing, she realized that she was as comfortable with Blake as she was with the guys in the lab. Who would have thought that an antisocial mathematician like her would get along with Mr. Perfect? "Tell me, Blake."

Blake looked down at her from his superior height. He'd shed his suit jacket and necktie. The sleeves of his white shirt were rolled up to the elbow, revealing muscular forearms. "I don't know where to start."

"The beginning?" Biting into an apple slice, she chewed with deliberation, refusing to be distracted by his masculine gorgeousness.

"Before he died, my dad sent me an e-mail. It was like a confession. He'd done something he regretted deeply."

"With Dr. Prentice?"

Blake paced on the worn Persian carpet in front of the desk. "Twenty-six years ago, on that army base near Roswell, Prentice was experimenting with frozen embryos. My mom was in her late thirties and thought she'd never have a baby. Prentice offered my father a solution."

He paused to pick up a framed photograph on the desk. "My mom never knew the truth about me. Biologically, I wasn't her child. I'm the result of an embryo created from two outstanding donors—people with high IQs and exceptional physical ability."

"Genetic engineering." That explained why Blake was so perfect. "Prentice was trying to create superbabies."

"Though he had ethical reservations, my dad agreed to monitor the experiment." He set down the photo and returned to the chair beside the sofa. "He measured the intellectual and psychological development of the supposed superbabies. Using subjects like you."

"Me?" she squeaked.

"You're highly intelligent. Your health is excellent."

"But I'm not perfect. All I have to do is look in a mirror to see that my mouth is too big. My nose has a weird curve at the tip. Besides, if I'm so genetically attractive, why don't I have a slew of boyfriends?"

"You've put all your energy into your intellect," he said. "When other girls were dating, you were studying."

She waved her hands to erase the memory of herself peering out from behind a stack of books to watch the other teenagers flirting and kissing in the library. Not that she'd been a recluse. She had gotten along well with guys and had had boyfriends. But there had always been something that got in the way. Her romantic life had been complicated to the point of nonexistence. "A truly superior specimen should be able to have it all."

"That's the part that fascinated my dad—the effects of nurturing and environment on subjects who started life with a genetic advantage."

"Wait." She hadn't even considered this angle. "If I was genetically engineered, the people who raised me aren't my biological parents. Did they know?"

"None of the parents knew. That was part of the study." He folded his arms across his chest and leaned against his father's desk. "You seem to be taking this well."

"In a sick way, it makes sense. Why not help nature along in the selection process? Why not make sure the most highly evolved people produce offspring?"

"Because it's wrong to manipulate people."

"It's morally shady," she said.

"It's fraud."

"But logical," she said. "Now I understand why Prentice impregnated me. He wants to create a second generation."

"What are you going to do now?"

"I don't know."

All she wanted was to get home, surround herself with silence and figure out how to restructure her life to accommodate a child.

Outside the office door, she heard other mourners arriving. They'd be eating, drinking and sharing memories of Dr. Ray, seeking solace in the company of others. Blake should be out there with his father's friends and colleagues. On the day of his father's funeral, he deserved closure.

She stood and straightened her shoulders. "I'm glad you told me, Blake. I don't blame your father. Not in the least. Dr. Ray was a good man."

"I know."

"Can I have my car keys? I need to go home."

He looked surprised. "I thought you were staying here tonight."

"Thanks for the offer, but I'd rather be alone."

"What about Prentice? I need to get in touch with him."

She took her cell phone from her purse, scanned her contacts and gave him the number for Dr. Prentice's private cell phone. "That's the best I can do."

As he handed over the keys, their hands touched. A spark of static electricity raced up her arm. She wondered if she'd ever see him again.

BLAKE STOOD ON THE PORCH and watched her drive away. He understood her need to be alone. When he had read the e-mail informing him that he wasn't biologically his father's son, Blake had felt as if somebody had punched him in the gut. Eve had a lot more to deal with. Finding out that she was pregnant without her consent or knowledge had to be a hell of a shock. Her life wasn't any of his business, but he hoped she wasn't considering adoption.

A couple of years ago, when he had been in college, his girlfriend had thought she might be pregnant. She'd knocked him for a loop. The only comparable feeling was when he had parachuted for the first time from fifteen thousand feet into enemy territory. He had known his life would be forever changed. That realization had been followed by an irrational sense of awe. Creating a new life? A miracle! When it had turned out to be a false alarm, his relief had mingled with deep regret.

He hoped that Eve would come to see her pregnancy in a positive light. No matter what she decided, he wouldn't abandon her. His dad's dying wish had been for him to take care of her.

Aunt Jean came out to the porch. "Are you coming inside?"

"I need to make a phone call first."

"Well, hurry up. People are asking about you."

His aunt meant well, as did his father's old friends. But Blake didn't see the point in mourning, not while the killer went free. That was why he needed to contact Prentice.

The cops had no leads in solving his dad's murder. They'd found no fingerprints or trace evidence. Because the burglar alarm had been expertly disabled and the safe robbed, they suspected a professional burglar.

Though Blake hadn't revealed the contents of his dad's e-mail, he had mentioned Prentice as a person with a grudge against his father. At his insistence, the homicide detective had spoken to Dr. Edgar Prentice—founder of the world-renowned Aspen IVF and Genetics Clinic in the mountains. Prentice's alibi was airtight; he'd been out of state at the time of the murder.

Of course, he'd cover his butt. Prentice would hire someone else to do his dirty work.

On his military cell phone that wouldn't give away his identity, Blake called the number Eve had given him. Prentice answered immediately. "Who is this?"

"Blake Jantzen. We need to talk."

"How did you get this number?"

"From Eve."

"Thank God you're with her."

Blake hadn't expected that response. The old bastard sounded as if he was concerned about Eve. "Why do you say that?"

"I might have inadvertently put her in danger. Stay with her, Blake. Your father would have wanted—"

"Don't talk to me about my father." *Unless you want to confess to his murder.*

"I should have called, should have made it to the funeral. I'm sorry. Sorry for your loss."

"Where are you?" Blake demanded. "I want to see you."

"That's not possible," Prentice said. "Stay with Eve. Make sure she's safe."

The call was disconnected.

Blake stared at his cell phone as if this piece of plastic and circuitry could tell him the truth. Either Prentice was lying to manipulate him or Eve was truly in danger. He couldn't take chances with her safety.

He ran down the driveway into the cul-de-sac where his father's station wagon was parked across the street. No time to waste. He started the engine.

Earlier, he'd planted a GPS locator on Eve's car in case he needed to find her. It'd be easy to follow her route on the hand-held tracking device he took from his pocket. Activating the system, he saw a reassuring blip. She was taking the back road to Boulder, avoiding traffic on the highway. Would she go to the lab where she worked? Or to her home?

His dad's station wagon wasn't a high performance vehicle, but after he got out of the burbs, he made good time on the two-lane road that ran parallel to the foothills. He passed a pickup and an SUV.

He never should have let her go, should have insisted that she stay at his house. If anything happened to her...

He passed a sedan that was already going over the speed limit. When he hit Boulder, the traffic slowed him down, but he was within a mile of her location when the tracking device showed that she'd parked.

The car in front of him at the stoplight rolled slowly forward. Blake wanted to honk, but he was back in mellow Colorado where car horns were seldom used. He turned right at the next corner and zipped the last few blocks to Eve's house.

Her car was parked at the curb in front of a yellow brick bungalow with a long front yard and mature shade trees on either side. Her unkempt shrubbery—spreading juniper and prickly clumps of potentilla—were good for xeriscaping but too plain for his taste. He preferred his mother's neatly pruned rose garden.

As soon as he opened his car door, he heard a scream.

Chapter Four

Eight minutes ago, Eve had unlocked her front door and entered her house, glad to be home. Her familiar surroundings had greeted her like old, faithful friends. The oversize wingback chair where she did most of her reading had beckoned, and she'd decided to curl up in its cozy embrace and have a cup of tea while her mind wrapped around the complications of being pregnant.

On the way to the kitchen to put on the hot water to boil, she'd patted the back of the comfy sofa with its multicolored throw pillows. She'd passed the round dining-room table.

In the doorway to the kitchen, she froze.

Two men, dressed in suits and neckties, stood between the sink and the refrigerator. Except for their sunglasses, they looked like businessmen at a sales meeting. She desperately wanted to believe that there was a logical reason for them to be here.

Holding her purse in front of her like a shield, she asked, "Who are you? How did you get into my house?"

"The back door was open."

That was probably true. She often forgot to lock up after leaving food for the feral cats that lived in the alley. Still, an unlocked door didn't constitute an invitation to enter. "What do you want?"

"Our employer wants to meet with you."

Were they talking about Prentice? "Who do you work for?"

With a cool smile, the taller man took a step toward her. If he lunged, he could grab her easily. That was when the reality of the situation hit her. These men were a threat.

"It's all right," he reassured her. "We aren't going to hurt you."

Liar! She was in severe danger, and she knew it. Her panicked instincts told her to run, but the men were bigger than she was. Faster. Stronger.

She had to be smarter.

Her mind cleared. She saw the problem as a geometric equation. Her kitchen was a rectangle with the two men in the center. She stood one step inside the doorway. To her left was a table and chairs. To her right, a cabinet jutted into the room. The distance between the corner of the cabinet and the corner of the kitchen table was approximately three feet. If she could block that space, she'd create an obstacle which would slow their pursuit and allow her to escape.

"Come with us, Eve." The tall man spoke in silky tones. "Everything will be explained to your satisfaction."

It took all her self-control to play along with his false civility. "This isn't convenient. Perhaps your employer could call me and make an appointment."

The second man drew a gun from a holster inside his jacket. "Enough playing around. Get over here."

A gun. Oh, God, he had a gun. "Don't shoot me."

Abruptly, she raised one hand over her head. When she lifted the other hand, she swung her arm wide. The tall man was forced to step back or be smacked by her purse. As he shifted his weight, she dropped both hands and yanked a chair from the table to block the three-foot space.

She pivoted and ran. Though she hadn't planned to scream, she heard herself wailing like a siren. Logic told her that she couldn't go faster than a bullet. Would they start shooting? Were they coming after her? She whipped open the front door—fortunately unlocked—and dashed outside. One step from the front stoop, she ran smack into Blake.

Though she was sprinting at full speed, she didn't knock him over. He staggered as he absorbed her velocity. "Are you all right?"

"Two men. One has a gun," she blurted. "We've got to get away."

He reacted forcefully. His left arm wrapped around her midsection, and he yanked her along with him. They were moving back toward the front door. *Wrong way!* They should be fleeing.

"He has a gun," she repeated.

"Heard you the first time."

His calm tone reminded her that he was a commando—specially trained to face danger. She could trust him. Though her pulse pounded and her nerve endings sizzled with fear, she forced herself to stand beside him on the porch instead of running willy-nilly toward her car. "What's next?" she asked.

"Stay."

"You mean, stay here?" She pointed to the concrete of the stoop. "Right here?"

Ignoring her, he was already on the move. He tore open the door to her house and charged inside, directly into the line of fire. His aggressive approach shocked her. He didn't have a weapon. How did he intend to overcome a man with a gun? *He's Special Forces,* she reminded herself. *His aggressive assault must be some sort of tactic.*

She pressed her back against the wall beside the mailbox

and clutched her purse against her chest. *Stay.* It was a simple, unambiguous command. But what if the men in suits left her kitchen and circled around to the front? What if Blake was shot? What if...

Oh, damn. She darted into the house behind him. In her clunky sandals, there was no way she could move stealthily, but she tried not to plod like a rhino. She went right—toward the bookshelves beside the fireplace where she grabbed a poker to use as a weapon. Then she hid behind her wingback reading chair. Peering around the arm, she saw no one. She heard no gunfire.

When Blake entered from the kitchen, his movements were as swift and efficient as a mountain lion on the prowl.

She popped up. "Are they gone?"

He went into attack mode. For a moment, she thought he was going to launch himself at her like a missile. Instead, he waved her toward him. "Come with me. Hurry."

Another quick command, spoken with authority. She jumped to obey. "I couldn't stay on the porch because—"

He grasped her arm and propelled her through the front door, off the porch and across the yard toward a station wagon. He ran around to the driver's side. "Get in."

She barely had time to fasten her seat belt before he was behind the wheel. He flipped the key in the ignition, and the station wagon roared down her quiet residential street like a tank.

"Keep your eyes open," he said. "Look for a black SUV with tinted windows."

"Where were they parked?"

"In the alley behind your house. I saw them pull away."

They were safe. She exhaled slowly, hoping to ease the

tension that clenched every muscle in her body. That brief encounter in her kitchen might have been the scariest thing that had ever happened to her. Though the confrontation only lasted eight minutes, it had felt like hours. According to Einstein, time was relative. Her fear made everything move in slow motion.

She reached into her purse and took out her cell phone. "I should call 911."

"Don't bother," he said. "Getting the cops involved is a waste of time."

Though she had no prior experience with intruders or guns being pointed at her, she was pretty sure he was wrong. "This is a job for the police."

"Did the intruders steal anything?"

"They weren't robbers."

"How do you know?"

"They knew my name and asked me to come with them."

"Not typical of burglars," he said.

"And they were wearing suits and neckties." She shuddered at the memory. "And gloves. The kind of throwaway latex gloves we wear in the lab if we're handling sensitive material."

"Did they break in?"

She frowned. "It wasn't exactly breaking and entering because my back door was unlocked, but they could be charged with…entering."

"You weren't harmed," he said. "What crime would you report to the police?"

"That guy pointed a gun at me. He's dangerous."

"You're right about that." He focused on the road, driving fast through a maze of residential streets. "They could be the men who killed my father."

The unexpectedness of his statement stunned her. The

air squeezed out of her lungs, and she felt herself gasping like a trout out of water. *Those men? Murderers?* She had it fixed in her mind that Dr. Ray was the victim of a burglary gone wrong—being in the wrong place at the wrong time. "You're saying that your father was targeted. That the murderer came after him on purpose. It was premeditated."

"Yes."

She waited for him to explain, but he was too busy watching in all directions and driving too fast. "Could you possibly be more terse?"

"No."

The tires squealed as Blake rounded a corner. "That's them. That's their vehicle."

At the foot of the hill in front of them, about two blocks away, she saw a black SUV. It made a left turn and disappeared from sight, thank goodness. Unless the bad guys doubled back, they were safe.

In a purely counterintuitive manner, Blake zoomed toward the other car. She shouted, "What are you doing?"

"Going after them."

He'd just acknowledged that those men were possibly murderers. "Are you crazy?"

"My dad was murdered. I have few leads and no evidence. Those guys might know something."

"Or they might kill us."

"Try to get the number on their license plate."

He hit the brakes to avoid a collision with a car pulling out of a driveway. At the corner, he had to stop again for schoolkids with backpacks crossing the street.

Finally reaching the corner, he turned in the direction the SUV had headed. This street fed into a main thoroughfare, and the other vehicle had already disappeared in traffic.

"Damn." Blake's right hand clenched into a fist which he pressed against his forehead. His jaw was tight. He winced, and the tiny creases at the corners of his eyes deepened.

She sensed the depth of his frustration. Though she had no desire to ever see either one of those men again, she said, "I'm sorry."

"Me, too."

Dozens of questions popped inside her head. Usually, Eve was good at sorting out variables and assigning rational values, but she didn't have enough information. "Why did you come to my house? Did you know I was in danger?"

"If I'd known, I never would have let you leave. I would never knowingly put you in harm's way."

His military phrasing reassured her; he sounded a bit like her father. "You must have had a reason for showing up on my doorstep."

He made another left turn and drove in the direction of her house. "I called Prentice to set up a meet, and he told me that he might have accidentally put you in danger."

"There are no accidents," she said darkly. If she hadn't been so confused, she would have been furious. Dr. Prentice was at the center of this tornado that had thrown her life into chaos. "Do you think Prentice is involved in your dad's murder?"

"I don't have facts or evidence," he said. "My dad's e-mail talked about the Prentice-Jantzen study. If he went public about the study, Prentice's reputation would be damaged. From what I've learned, the Aspen IVF and Genetics Clinic is big business."

"So your father was a threat."

Blake nodded. "His files pertaining to the study are missing, probably stolen."

"Did the police question Prentice?"

"He has an alibi."

But he could have hired those two men in suits. "You should have told me your suspicions about your father's murder. There's no logical reason for you to withhold information."

He pulled up to a stop sign and turned toward her. His gaze seemed to soften as he placed his hand on her shoulder. "I didn't say anything about the murder because I thought you'd had enough shocks for one day."

"True enough." Finding out that she was pregnant and that her mom and dad weren't her genetic parents were huge issues. "Nonetheless, it might have been useful to know about the potential for danger."

"Don't worry." His voice was gentle. "I won't let anything bad happen to you."

His touch warmed her through the cotton fabric of her jacket as he massaged her shoulder. He gave a light squeeze before turning back toward the road.

While she continued to stare at his perfect profile, the questions inside her head turned to gibberish. She wanted him to hold her and comfort her and tell her that everything was going to be all right. Their brief physical contact had erased her intelligence like a bucket of white paint thrown against a blackboard filled with equations. With one pat on her shoulder, he'd turned her into a dumb blonde.

"When we get back to your house," he said, "I want you to pack a suitcase. You'll be staying with me."

She couldn't put her life on hold. There were important projects at work—schedules to be met and responsibilities to be handled. Though she should have been telling him all those things, all she could manage to say was, "Okay."

Staying with Blake seemed like the most rational plan she'd heard all day.

BACK AT HER HOUSE, Blake stood in the center of her kitchen, which was incredibly clean. Either she was a neat freak or she didn't actually cook. He suspected the latter. He faced her. "I want to reenact what happened while your memory is fresh. They were standing here, right?"

"The shorter one was there. The tall guy was closer." She motioned him toward her. "Move eighteen inches forward."

He did so. "Here?"

"Close enough."

As she explained what had happened, using geometry analogies, he cursed himself for missing his chance to nab these two guys. He should have been faster, should have driven her home and entered her house first.

She pulled the chair down onto the floor and concluded, "Then I ran. And screamed."

"And they didn't come after you?"

Her chin lifted. "Apparently, I outsmarted them by creating an effective obstacle."

Though he had no doubt that her IQ was double that of these two characters, an overturned chair wasn't all that impressive. He motioned for her to start running. "Go ahead and show me what you did next."

When she darted toward the front door, he hurdled the chair. Before her hand was on the doorknob, he caught her arm and spun her around to face him.

Her blue eyes widened as she leaned her back against the closed door and gazed up at him. "You got me."

"And I wasn't even running hard."

"I can explain," she said. "You were ready to chase me, and they weren't. Plus you're taller than them. Longer legs mean you're faster. Or maybe I wasn't moving as fast."

"Or maybe those two guys were incompetent."

They'd taken off like a couple of scared jackrabbits as

soon as they'd realized she wasn't alone. He would have thought Prentice could afford a better grade of thug.

"I still think we should talk to the police," Eve said. "I can identify both of those men. I'm very observant."

"Prove it."

"The taller man was five feet eleven inches tall. He had a gold pinkie ring with an amber stone and his watch had a gold and silver band. Cleft chin. Small ears. High forehead. The other one probably put on some weight recently because the waistband on his trousers was tight."

He watched her lips as she rattled off more details about their shoes and shirts and the cut of their hair. He could have stepped back and given her more space, but he liked being close. "You have a photographic memory."

"It's called eidetic memory or recall, and I'm not one hundred percent. But I'm good with visuals and numbers." She reached toward him and rested the flat of her palm against his chest. "It's a useful skill, especially for investigating. I'm sure we'll find the man who killed your father."

"We?"

"You and me," she said. "With your Special Forces training and my logic, we'll make a really good team."

This plan had to be nipped in the bud. He caught hold of her hand and gently lowered it to her side. No way did he intend to get tied down with a partnership. This was his fight. "I appreciate the offer, but no."

"Why not?"

"The situation is dangerous." He moved away from her. "While I'm investigating, I can't be worried about what's happening to you."

"But you want me to come home with you," she said. "To stay at your house. What am I supposed to be doing while you're investigating?"

His father's last wish was for him to protect Eve. He couldn't put her in jeopardy. "Maybe you could take up knitting."

"And maybe you could go to hell."

"Too late, babe. I'm already there."

"Don't call me babe."

Her eyes flared with righteous anger. He didn't blame her for being ticked off. He hadn't been gentle in rejecting her, but he didn't have time to waste. Clues were fading like footprints on a beach being washed away by the tide. He needed to focus on finding his father's killer. "Pack your things."

"Tell you what, Blake. I'm going to let your condescending, sexist attitude slide for now because I know you're under duress. But make no mistake. My abilities are a valuable resource. You need me."

He watched as she moved past him and turned into the hallway. She was smart, all right. But, in this case, she was wrong. He had never in his life needed anyone.

Chapter Five

No matter how irritated she got, Eve had to accept the fact that Blake was well-trained for situations involving physical violence, and she'd be wise to follow his directions. Still, she didn't want to be totally dependent on him and definitely wanted to have access to her own car while she was staying at his father's house.

When he loaded her suitcase into the back of his station wagon, she said, "I'll drive myself and meet you there."

He slammed the car door closed. "Ever been in a high-speed pursuit?"

"No."

"Do you have training in evasive driving tactics?"

She could see where he was heading. Her shoulders slumped, and she exhaled a sigh. "I'm pretty good at dodging squirrels."

"If those guys see you driving alone, they might try to apprehend you again." He gave her a wink. "You ride with me."

She groaned. Her life had become too dangerous for her to drive her own car. Too dangerous to sleep in her own bed. This was so unfair. When she glanced over her shoulder at her cozy little bungalow with the warm brown bricks and the clean white trim at the windows, an unwanted memory of fear tightened her gut. Those intruders had invaded her privacy, violated her home. Never before had she felt so vulnerable. She wanted bars on the windows and triple locks on the doors. Even then, she didn't know if she'd feel secure. "There's something I need to do before we leave."

She marched up the sidewalk to the front door and went through the living room and dining room to the kitchen where she took a bag of dried cat food from the cupboard. The stray cats in the alley depended on her for food. She couldn't abandon them. Nor could she leave the whole bag by the trash cans in the alley where the raccoons would carry it off.

Later she'd call her neighbor and ask him to take over for her while she was away. And how long would that be? A day? A week? Two weeks? So unfair!

As she went out the back door and down the narrow sidewalk to the gate in the white picket fence, Blake followed. "What are you doing?"

"Taking care of the wildlife. There's a family of cats that live out here."

Instead of scoffing, he spoke in a gentle voice. "You could call animal rescue. I'm sure there are organizations that take care of feral animals."

"I've tried." Four times she'd contacted humane groups. "These little guys don't want to be caught. Even when the cat rescue people manage to pick up one or two, another litter of kittens appears. They multiply like Tribbles."

"Like what?"

She squatted beside a blooming lilac bush and poured cat food into a plastic container. "Tribbles. You know, furry critters that reproduce exponentially. From *Star Trek*."

"You're a Trekkie," he said. "That explains the T-shirt."

When she'd changed out of her too-short skirt, she had

put on black denim jeans and the least obnoxious T-shirt in her closet—blue with a subtle Enterprise emblem above her left breast. If she slipped back into her black jacket, no one would notice the emblem.

"I'm not a psycho fan," she said. "But I've attended a number of science fiction and fantasy cons. You'd probably like them. G.I. Joe is popular again."

As she watched, two gray-striped kittens peeked over the low-hanging lilac boughs and mewed.

"Hi, little guys."

Eve sat back on her heels so she wouldn't scare them. The kittens crept closer to the food, nudging each other. Their yellow eyes were huge in their tiny faces. Their pink noses pushed at the dry food.

Blake squatted beside her. "New members of the feral cat family?"

"I've never seen these two before." The way she figured, there must be a couple of females who were constantly pregnant—no need for frozen embryos with these felines. "Tribbles."

One of the kittens jumped and scurried back into the bushes. The other sat and stared at Eve. A brave little one. Would her child be courageous? And curious?

Slowly, she stretched out her hand, palm up, toward the kitten. The pink nose came closer and closer. With sharp little claws, the kitten batted at her finger, then darted away.

Babies—kittens, puppies and people—had the most remarkable innocence. And so much to learn. Would she be a good teacher? A good mother? Damn it, she couldn't even take care of herself, much less a baby.

Tears welled up, and she bolted to her feet so Blake wouldn't notice that she was crying. He already regarded her as less than useful in terms of his investigation, and she didn't want him to add weepy to his list of complaints.

During the ride back to Denver, she intended to convince him that she ought to be his partner. It was only logical: two minds were better than one.

Sitting in the passenger seat, she waited to speak until they were on the highway and relatively free from the distraction of stop-and-go traffic. Without preface she said, "If Prentice warned you that I was in danger, he must have wanted you to protect me. Therefore, it's unlikely that he sent those two intruders."

Blake stared through the windshield, refusing to respond.

She continued, "Prentice also said that he might have accidentally caused the threat, which implies that he knows who sent them."

Though he still didn't comment, a muscle in his jaw twitched.

"And so," she said, "Prentice must have communicated with someone after he spoke to me. Is there any way we can get his phone records? Or monitor his e-mails?"

Grudgingly, Blake said, "I can't reach him. He won't answer the phone when I call. Supposedly, he's on vacation."

"He talked to me."

"I seriously doubt that he'll set up a meeting with you."

"Probably not." Their conversation hadn't been friendly. "He can't just disappear. Someone at his clinic in Aspen must know where he is."

"They won't rat out their employer. Even if we find him, he's smart enough to use an untraceable phone or encrypted computer."

They were sharing information, and that pleased her. As

long as she didn't talk about his father, she figured Blake would work with her. "When I talked to him, his voice got tense when I hinted that I might give the baby up for adoption. For some reason, Prentice and the person who sent the intruders want me to be a real mother and raise this child. I'd like to find out who was working on this study."

"You think another scientist wants to continue the experiment through you."

"It's possible," she conceded.

But genetic engineering—both the concept and the practice—had greatly evolved over the past twenty-five years. The Prentice-Jantzen study was archaic when compared with new research on the human genome. It simply didn't make scientific sense to continue with an outmoded methodology. "If I give birth to the second generation, who benefits?"

"The father."

His quick response surprised her, though it shouldn't have. The existence of a male sperm donor was, of course, necessary to create a viable embryo. But she had avoided thinking about that part of the equation.

If her child truly was second generation, the father had to be someone else in the initial study. They needed to know the identities of the original superbabies. "We need to see your father's notes on the Prentice-Jantzen study."

"Can't," he said. "That data was stolen in the robbery."

Dr. Ray was murdered and his notes stolen. Surely, not a coincidence.

BY THE TIME THEY GOT BACK to Denver, sunset had colored the skies with fiery red and yellow. A few years ago in Kenya, Blake had seen the body of an elder burned on a funeral pyre in a solemn ceremony. The flames purified and released the soul from the body.

He had buried his father today. And yet, he felt no sense of closure.

Outside his father's house, only a few extra cars were parked on the cul-de-sac. Apparently, most of the mourners had already paid their respects and gone home. "We'll leave your suitcase in the car. It's easier than explaining. I'm pretty sure that Aunt Jean won't approve of you spending the night."

"If you're worried about your reputation," she said coolly, "I'd be happy to tell your aunt that there's no hanky-panky going on."

"Just don't say anything."

"Yes, sir."

She snapped off a sarcastic salute. Oh, yeah, Eve was definitely an army brat. Also a math nerd and genetic genius. And pregnant. His dad had picked one hell of a difficult woman for him to protect.

When he opened the front door for her, he heard *Rhapsody in Blue* being played on the grand piano in the living room. He took two steps on the polished hardwood floor before the music stopped him like an invisible wall of sound. The gliding crescendos held bittersweet memories. "This is one of my dad's favorites."

"Dr. Ray had good taste."

His mom had been the real musician in the family. Almost every day, she practiced at the piano, sometimes Mozart but more often Cole Porter tunes. His dad loved to sing along. Blake remembered the two of them sitting on the piano bench, humming and laughing.

When he was growing up, Mom had tried to include him in their music. First, by teaching him the basics, which he stumbled through. Then, she had learned songs she thought he'd like. He smiled at the memory of her playing Backstreet Boys and Busta Rhymes while she had rapped in her angelic soprano voice.

After she had died, his dad's life had been greatly diminished. Blake should have made more of an effort to get home and spend time with him. Under his breath, he said, "I could have been a better son."

"The down and dirty truth," Eve murmured.

"Did he talk to you about me?"

"He loved you and was proud of you." She tossed her head and her blond hair bounced. "But when you said that you could be better, that was true. Human behavior can always be improved upon."

"Not like math, huh? Numbers are perfect."

Her eyebrows lifted. "You really don't want to get me started on this topic."

The musical selection concluded, and they went into the front room. Seven people stood beside the gleaming rosewood instrument, applauding the pianist. Among the audience, Blake recognized General Stephen Walsh. His close-cropped white hair stood at attention. The array of medals and decorations—evidence of a long, heroic career—dated back to Vietnam when he was an enlisted man. Though General Walsh and his father hadn't seen eye to eye on the treatment of post-traumatic stress disorder in veterans, they had remained friends and occasional golf partners. Walsh was a good man to have as an ally.

The pianist was David Vargas. Blake had only met David briefly but suspected that he might be another of the superbabies in the Prentice-Jantzen Study.

His aunt swooped toward him. "Where on earth have you been? Everyone has been asking about you."

When he introduced Aunt Jean to Eve, his aunt eyed her

casual black denim pants and loafers with disdain. "I saw you at the funeral. And you were at the house earlier."

"I had to leave because I was feeling ill." Eve pulled her black jacket to cover the Trekkie symbol on her T-shirt. "I changed clothes and I'm much better now. Looks like you could use some help putting away the food from the buffet table."

"I certainly could." Aunt Jean smoothed her soft brown hair into the bun at the nape of her long neck. "I'd like to pack most of this up and take it downtown to a mission my church runs. Is that all right with you, Blakey?"

"Sure." He couldn't remember if he'd eaten today. Must have. Aunt Jean had been pushing food at him since he got out of bed.

As the two women carried plates into the kitchen, Blake approached David Vargas, who stood beside the piano.

"You play well," he said. "Professional musician?"

"Music is my hobby," Vargas said. "A way to relax."

He was a sharp dresser—smooth and classy without trying too hard. Though he appeared to be the same age as Blake, his black hair had a streak of white at the right temple. His eyes gleamed like silver dollars.

"How did you know my dad?" Blake asked.

"I was part of a study he did with Dr. Prentice."

Blake's first impression had been correct. "How much do you know about the study?"

"Quite a lot. In my teens, I had an illness that might have been genetic. When my parents consulted with Prentice, I discovered that we didn't share the same DNA."

Blake wondered how many of the others had known the truth about their conception. "Did you learn the identities of your biological parents?"

"Unfortunately, no. It turned out that my illness wasn't

serious and not caused by my DNA. There was no need to track them down."

"Did you continue with the study?"

"I did. I'd like to say that I was motivated by intellectual curiosity, but your father pointed out an emotional reason. He said I have a need for belonging, family and heritage. Though I don't share identical DNA with the other subjects, it felt like we're related, like I have brothers and sisters."

Blake hadn't considered that perspective. Though an only child, he'd never lacked for companions, male and female. When he had joined the army and gone into Special Forces, the men in his platoon had become his brothers. "Did my dad give you any information about the others?"

"He was discreet," Vargas said. "But I'm guessing that you and I share a similar birth history."

"Correct."

They exchanged an assessing gaze. Blake was a couple of inches taller and carried fifteen pounds more muscle. If it ever came to a physical fight between them, he had the clear advantage.

He wondered how Vargas had used his genetic gifts. His clothes were too expensive for an academic, so he probably hadn't gone into teaching or research. Though he held himself with the confidence of a surgeon, he had the kind of charisma that came from working with other people.

"Finance," Vargas said, answering his unspoken question. "I made my first million before I was twenty. Our current economy makes for some fascinating challenges."

"But you're doing okay."

"More than okay."

"Good for you." He didn't want to get competitive,

but he also didn't want to hear about a balance sheet that showed billions in profit.

Vargas glanced toward the buffet table where Eve was trying to carry three casserole dishes at the same time. "What about her? What's her story?"

Blake watched Eve's balancing act, which was definitely not an example of genius. She'd already smeared a glob of melted cheese on the front of her Trekkie T-shirt. "What makes you think she's one of us?"

"Playing the odds. She's the right age and must have had a relationship with your father. What does she do?"

"Mathematician. She works at Sun Wave Labs in Boulder."

"You came in together," Vargas said. "Are you dating?"

"Me and Eve? No." *Hell, no.*

He straightened his shirt collar. "I'd like to get to know her better. Do you mind?"

Hell, yes. Blake's gut clenched. *Back off, Finance Man.* But he had no claim on Eve. "She's all yours."

As he watched, David Vargas moved in like a python coiling around its prey. No way in hell could Eve handle this super-rich, super-charming guy. He'd sweep her off her loafers.

Blake felt as if he should warn her, but Eve's affections weren't his problem. He took his cell phone from his pocket and placed a call to the homicide detective investigating his father's murder. Might as well report the break-in at Eve's house. The detective might get useful fingerprints.

He heard Eve giggle as she talked to Vargas. Blake had no right to feel possessive about her, but he was secretly glad that she'd be spending the night here at his house. Far away from Vargas.

Chapter Six

Eve stood under the light on the porch and watched as David Vargas pulled away from the curb. His hybrid SUV was packed with floral arrangements that he'd promised to drop off at local hospitals and nursing homes, but she really didn't think he'd make those deliveries himself. Vargas presented himself as a very important guy—a legend in his own mind—who had battalions of assistants to take care of life's pesky details.

When he had first started talking to her and helping her clear the buffet table, she'd been puzzled. Why would somebody like him—a rich and powerful mover and shaker—show interest in somebody like her? Guys like Vargas dated supermodels. Why would he waste his considerable charm on a mathematician in a Star Trek T-shirt?

Not being one for subtlety, she'd asked him point-blank. "Why?"

"The Prentice-Jantzen study," he'd said without losing a glimmer of his suavity. "I believe we were both subjects."

Did Blake know about this? She'd wanted to signal him, but he had been deep in conversation with the general. "How much have you found out about the study?"

"Enough to know that we're genetically superior. You and I are unique."

"Except for the others."

"There were twenty-four subjects," he had said. "Only two women."

She'd filed away that bit of information for future reference. "Do you know any of the others?"

"Just you and Blake." The overhead light had glistened on the streak of silver in his hair. "And I only figured that out today when I saw you both at the funeral. You're the right age. You had a connection to Dr. Ray. And there's something remarkable about you."

"Me? I don't think so." There was nothing special about her, except for the pregnant virgin bit.

"I'd like to see you again, Eve."

"Give me a call."

"I will," he had promised.

Apparently, her genetically engineered birth made her a hottie. Might be nice to have Vargas fawning over her. She could do a lot worse than dating a handsome, intelligent, wealthy, musically gifted man.

Aunt Jean bustled outside with her purse slung over her shoulder and her jacket tucked under her arm. "I need to get going before all this food turns bad. Will you be all right?"

"I'm fine." Eve remembered that Blake hadn't wanted his aunt to know she was spending the night. "I'll get Blake to drive me home later."

"I'm worried about him. Losing his father like this, well, it's hard." She made a tsk-tsk noise. "Our Blakey is so big and strong we sometimes forget that he has a sensitive streak. Like his mother."

Though Eve hadn't seen much evidence of sensitivity

in Blake, she didn't object. "It's hard on you, too. Losing a brother."

"Ray and I weren't close. He was ten years older than me." Her lips pinched together, and Eve had the impression that Aunt Jean would have had quite a bit to say if she'd been the sort of woman who spoke ill of the dead. "I'll pray for my brother. And for Blakey. He's the only family I've got left."

He should have been out here on the porch, saying a proper goodbye to his aunt. "I wonder where he's disappeared to."

"He was always like that. Going off by himself." She patted Eve on the arm. "See if you can get him to open up."

Eve seriously doubted that was going to happen. Blake held himself like a closed fist.

After Jean left, she went back into the house and closed the door. With Dr. Ray gone, no one really lived here anymore. The house felt desolate. "Blake?"

If he wanted to slink off by himself, fine with her. But he was supposed to be her bodyguard. If somebody tried to break in, she was totally unprotected.

Her footfalls echoed on the hardwood floor as she went through the living room, turning on the lights that Jean had just extinguished. Where was he? She needed to talk to him, to get this investigation rolling.

On the granite countertop in the kitchen, she found the brown leather condolence book that guests had signed at the funeral service and at the reception. Several pages were filled with signatures and brief remembrances.

Tucked into the back of the book was a note from Aunt Jean. At the top, she'd written emphatically: "Blake, send thank-you cards." Then came a list of names of those who had brought flowers or casseroles. Eve's mother would have done exactly the same thing. It was protocol.

Eve had a different take on the condolence book. Some of the people who had signed could be suspects. She started at the top of the first page and scanned all the names, committing them to memory. Vargas had a strong, dramatic scrawl. General Walsh's handwriting was shaky, causing her to wonder about the state of his health. Someone named Peter Gregory added an odd comment: "Rock on, Dr. Ray." There was another Gregory. Peter's father? Her eyes stopped on Dr. Trevor Latimer. She'd seen that name listed outside the clinic where Prentice had taken her for the supposed examination when he had implanted the embryo.

She knew the clinic address but not the phone number. When she'd arrived to meet Prentice, it had been after closing time. No one but Prentice and his assistant had been there. That clinic might be a good starting point for their investigation.

With the book in hand, she prowled down the hallway toward Dr. Ray's office. No doubt, he had an address file in here. She could start researching these other names.

When she opened the door, she saw Blake sitting on the leather sofa. He was hunched over, elbows on knees, staring into a glass of amber liquid. He drained the dregs and poured more whiskey from an open bottle on the coffee table in front of him. "Are they gone?"

She could have given him a hard time for not treating his aunt with the proper respect, but she could see that he was already doing a fine job of beating himself up. "Everybody's left."

He glared at her with bloodshot eyes. "Even your boyfriend?"

"Who?"

"The financial whiz kid." His upper lip curled in a sneer. "Vargas."

"For your information, Vargas is one of us, one of the superbabies. And he seems to know about the study. Maybe he can help us investigate."

"You and I aren't investigating together. I'm doing this alone."

She thought they'd already gotten around this barrier. "I don't mind you being stubborn, but don't be a jerk. I can't help being involved. Men with guns broke into my house."

"Stubborn, huh?"

"And a jerk."

He rose to his feet, snatched the tumbler and took another aggressive gulp. "You didn't tell Vargas my suspicions about the murder, did you?"

"Give me some credit." She knew a thing or two about strategy. "I know better than to blab. Loose lips sink ships."

"Well said, army brat."

She'd seen her share of troops coming home from battle, struggling for control. Blake was on the edge. He'd buried his father today, and he was deeply troubled by the murder.

She needed for him to focus. Holding up the condolence book, she said, "I have a lead. I started going through the names of people who came to the funeral and—"

"Vargas is the kind of guy who needs to be in charge. He's the boss man."

Not unlike Blake. Both he and David Vargas were alpha males—intelligent and charismatic. Both were natural leaders. "Are you jealous?"

"Of him? No way. Well, maybe I'd like to know his tailor. Or his barber." With his finger, Blake drew a line on his temple. "Maybe I should get myself a silver streak. Skunk hair."

She slammed the condolence book down on the coffee table. The resulting thud was loud enough to compel Blake's attention. Though she empathized with his need to mourn, they didn't have time for self-pity.

Circling the coffee table, she stood before him. "You need to shape up. And we'll start by pouring a gallon of coffee down your throat."

"What if I don't want coffee?" He leaned toward her. "Are you going to make me drink it?"

"Oh. Hell. Yes."

His nose was six inches away from hers. She stared into his chocolate-brown eyes and saw a subtle shift. He was looking at her with a strange awareness, as if really seeing her for the first time, as if he liked what he saw.

He actually licked his lips. His right hand slipped around her waist. First Vargas. Now Blake. What was going on here? Was she exuding some kind of irresistible pheromone?

She could have moved away, could have resisted.

But when he pulled her close, she melted into his embrace.

Never before had she been kissed like this. Though she was a virgin, she had enough experience to know what it meant to be aroused. Her blood rushed. Her pulse rate accelerated. Goose bumps shivered up and down her arms and thighs.

Blake held her tight, tilting her so her back arched slightly. His hand cupped her bottom and merged her loins with his. When she rubbed against him, the friction generated waves of heat that spread like an atomic reaction and exploded, not with a bang but a whoosh, like a prolonged sigh.

His other arm angled around her upper body and pulled

her tighter, so tight that her breasts crushed against his hard, muscled chest.

His mouth tasted of whiskey, an exotic flavor that she usually didn't care for. This taste was different, and she loved the sharp tang, couldn't get enough. Hungrily, she parted her lips and drew his tongue into her mouth.

Her senses heightened. She ran her fingers through his hair and reveled in the exquisite texture. His mysterious, utterly masculine aroma tantalized her nostrils. Her ears rang with precisely tuned chimes. Each note vibrated through her.

When her eyelids opened, she was dazzled by his perfect features. She inhaled his breath, drew it deep inside her lungs. She was meant to be joined with Blake. He was the man she'd been waiting for.

His grasp loosened.

She stepped backward. Still caught up in the pure pleasure of his kiss, she was unable to function normally. She couldn't speak, couldn't think. Her mind—usually sharp and clear—blurred in wonderful confusion.

Struggling to regain her equilibrium, she tried to choke out a coherent sentence. "We should, um, do something. I think. Do you?"

"Absolutely," he said.

She could tell by the flush of color on his cheeks and his grin that he'd been similarly affected by their kiss. But Blake had an excuse. He was half-drunk.

"Coffee," she said, grasping at the threads of reality.

Before she could float from the room, he grounded her with a statement of fact. "I talked to the homicide detective looking into my father's murder."

The importance of their investigation paled when compared to that incredible kiss. "Uh-huh."

"He's going to your house in Boulder. The crime scene investigators will look for forensic evidence."

The facts pierced her romantic haze like darts into a balloon. Her sensual epiphany began to deflate. "They won't find fingerprints. The men were wearing gloves."

"There might be a hair. A footprint." His gaze turned toward his father's desk. "They didn't find anything useful in here."

Back to earth, she realized that they were standing in the middle of a crime scene. The other time she'd been in his father's office she hadn't been paying attention. Her thoughts had been too distracted by finding out she was pregnant. "What were you doing in this room?"

"For one thing," he said, "my aunt refuses to come in here."

"Cut her some slack. Aunt Jean is a nice woman."

"I know. And I'm glad she's praying for me."

He didn't look glad. His features had become as rigid as Mount Rushmore. In less than a minute, he'd gone from "at ease" to strict "attention." His chin pulled back. His spine was ramrod stiff. It didn't seem possible for him to erase the passion they'd shared so quickly. "Was there another reason you came in here?"

"The whiskey bottle in the lower desk drawer," he admitted. "And I wanted to visualize what happened. Recreate the scene."

"Like we did at my house." She moved toward the windows, giving herself a wider perspective. *Don't think about sex. It's not appropriate.* "Tell me about the forensic evidence."

"As if you were my partner."

"Exactly."

Grudgingly, he said, "My father was seated behind the

desk. Shot three times in the chest. He had a gun in his hand."

"Was his gun fired?"

"Four times."

Blake pointed out the bullet holes in the wall. The pitted marks, circled in black to facilitate forensic photos, were above the framed photographs on the wall. Almost at the ceiling. Either Dr. Ray was a terrible marksman or he hadn't been trying to hit his target.

She asked, "Signs of a struggle?"

"None."

"Do you have a theory about what happened?"

He stepped away from the sofa and stood beside her. When his arm came close to hers, he leaned away, almost as if he wanted to avoid touching.

"Shortly before he was murdered, Dad sent me an e-mail, which explains why he was at the desk. The person who broke in bypassed the alarm system."

"Suggesting a professional burglar." She glanced at the wall safe behind the desk. The heavy door stood ajar. "What happened to the contents of the safe?"

"Gone."

Eve understood why the police suspected a burglary gone wrong. The evidence indicated that an armed intruder had disabled the security to enter the house and proceeded to the office with the intention of robbing the safe. "Did he keep valuables in there?"

"Not to my knowledge," he said. "The safe was for important documents, like deeds and investment information. Since all his information on the Prentice study is missing, I suspect those papers were in the safe."

That was why he'd said his father's research was stolen. "Was anything else taken?"

"His laptop."

Seeking a different visual angle, she went behind the desk. In spite of the clutter, she discerned an order. Unopened mail and magazines were on the left side. The file folders and papers on the right showed signs of use. A framed photograph of Blake and his mother leaned against those piles.

Blood stained the leather chair and the worn Persian carpet. Splatters dotted the desktop clutter in an irregular pattern. "Some of these files have been moved."

"I've shuffled through these papers. Nothing of interest. Mostly, it's outdated correspondence and notes from conferences. No patient files."

"Where did he keep his patient files?"

"At his office downtown. He shares space with a couple of other shrinks. I've already been there to search for the Prentice-Jantzen research."

"What about patient confidentiality? I'm surprised they'd let you go through the files."

"They didn't," he said. "But I stood over the secretary's shoulder as she flipped through documents and scanned the computer."

She noticed that the center area of the desk was cleared; that must have been where Dr. Ray placed his laptop. Without touching, she leaned down to examine the surface which was dotted with blood. "Apparently, he moved his laptop before he was shot."

"Why do you think so?"

"If the laptop had been on the desk, there would have been a blank space in the spatters."

"Good observation."

"Suppose he put the laptop in the safe," she said, "because he knew it contained valuable information—data that he didn't want to fall into the wrong hands."

"Which meant that he knew someone was after it." His

voice took on an edge of enthusiasm. "My dad was aware of the threat. He knew they were coming for him."

Now they were getting somewhere. "What else can you tell me about the forensic evidence?"

"He was shot in the heart. His death was almost instantaneous. Which means he wouldn't have had time to retaliate with four shots."

She drew the logical conclusion. "Dr. Ray fired first. Before he was hit."

"And he aimed high."

The logical action when being attacked would have been to shoot directly at your assailant. "What might cause your father to sit at his desk and fire four shots toward the ceiling?"

"Maybe he heard the intruder in the hallway and fired his gun to warn him off. Before he was hit, he had enough time to punch the speed dial and alert the security company."

Without sitting in the bloodstained desk chair, she pantomimed those actions. First, she pretended to hit the button on the phone, then she cocked her finger like a gun. "Like this. Bang, bang, bang, bang."

Blake moved to the doorway, playing the role of the assassin. "The killer steps inside and shoots."

"But if your father knew he was being attacked, he would have ducked behind the desk for cover."

"Unless he recognized his attacker. That might have caused him to pause for a fatal few seconds."

Their logic was beginning to create a complete picture. "He hides his laptop in the safe. Then, he hears an intruder, calls security and fires warning shots. Then he stops himself from shooting when he sees someone he knows. The killer wasn't an anonymous intruder or a burglar or even a hitman. This was someone he recognized. A coworker. Or a patient."

"Or someone he'd known from birth," Blake said darkly. "One of the subjects from the study."

Someone like them. A highly intelligent individual bent on murder.

Chapter Seven

In the kitchen, Blake leaned against the oak cabinets and watched as Eve precisely measured coffee grounds and poured them into the basket of the coffeemaker. She'd taken off her shoes, revealing slender, well-shaped feet. He had to wonder what the rest of her body looked like under the shapeless Trekkie T-shirt and loose-fitting denim slacks.

She sure as hell didn't work at being attractive. Hers was an unintentional beauty. Potent, nonetheless. Damn it, he shouldn't have kissed her. That was just plain wrong.

"Do you think half a pot is enough?" she asked.

"Doesn't matter." He wished that she'd stop treating him like a drunk. It took more than a couple of shots to affect him. "Coffee doesn't really sober you up."

"Is that the voice of experience talking?"

"The only real effect of caffeine on alcohol is to make you a more wide-awake drunk."

"I'll settle for wide-awake." She turned on the coffeemaker and faced him. "Are there any security measures we should be taking?"

"I turned on the burglar alarm."

"The same system that the killer disconnected before?"

"This is an upgrade." The security company had been

apologetic about the failure of their equipment and had installed a state-of-the-art digital system that supposedly couldn't be breached without setting off buzzers. Still, she had a point. Blake knew better than to trust everything to technology. "Plus, you've got me as a bodyguard."

Her wide mouth stretched in a grin. "Is that supposed to be reassuring?"

"Seriously, Eve. I can protect you."

"Seriously? You're not armed."

Actually, that wasn't true. He'd borrowed a handgun from the general, which he'd hidden under the pillows in his bedroom. He didn't need an arsenal to protect her, and she needed to understand that. "I always carry a knife."

She challenged him, "Are you any good with it?"

He whirled, grasped the handle of a butcher knife in a block on the counter, pulled it and threw. The blade stuck in the oak door frame, exactly where he'd been aiming. "How's that?"

"You made your point." She shrugged. "No pun intended."

Her nonchalance was annoying; he'd been going for shock and awe. "Come on, Eve. That was one hell of an impressive display. At least give me an 'atta boy.'"

"Can you show me how to do it?"

"Depends. How's your coordination?"

"Not bad." She padded across the tiled kitchen floor to the refrigerator. The shelves inside were packed with plastic containers of leftovers. In the crisper, she found a bag of oranges which she scattered on the countertop. Giving him a smirk, she started juggling a couple of them.

"Only two?"

"Getting warmed up."

She added a third orange. Her concentration was intense.

The tip of her tongue poked against her lower lip as she rotated the oranges in the air. Damn, she was cute.

"How about four?" he teased.

"Three's good." Her hips swayed in rhythm with the motion of her arms. "I only do prime numbers."

"Like five," he said.

"Think you can outdo me?"

She tossed the oranges to him, one at a time. Without missing a beat, he continued to juggle. Three were easy. When she flipped a fourth toward him, he worked it in.

"Atta boy," she said as she opened the refrigerator door again.

In his peripheral vision, he saw her take something else from the fridge. A small white oval. An egg.

Before she could throw it, he stopped juggling, allowing the oranges to thud to the floor. He stepped forward, took both her hands and squeezed them around the egg. The shell cracked but nothing oozed out.

"Hard-boiled," she said, looking up at him with mischief in her eyes. "I put them away when I was helping your aunt. Did you really think I'd pelt you with a raw egg?"

"The thought crossed my mind."

That wasn't the only thing he was thinking. Standing close to her, he remembered the way her body had molded against his. She'd felt too good in his arms; it couldn't happen again.

He forced himself to release her hands. Pacing across the floor, he yanked the blade from the door frame and returned it to the butcher block. "Since you're the target, it's probably best if we sleep in the same room."

Though her grin didn't slip, her eyes widened. He imagined that she was calculating her response. "What are you suggesting?"

"Sleep," he said. "Anything more would be wrong."

"Wrong?" Her smile vanished. "That seems like a strong word."

Their kiss in his father's office was a mistake. He hadn't considered the ramifications. Apparently, neither had she.

When he looked into her lovely, intelligent blue eyes, the heat in the kitchen shot up by several degrees. The delicious aroma of freshly brewing coffee swirled around them. If he reached out, he could touch her, pull her close against him. He was physically attracted to her. And he shouldn't be.

"Genetically," he said, "we might be brother and sister."

Her brother? Eve stared at him with a mixture of disbelief and disgust. Had she kissed her brother? And enjoyed it? "You're creeping me out, Blake."

"Think about it. Prentice drew from a limited number of volunteers. They had to meet certain requirements in terms of physical health, mental acuity and fertility. The testing wasn't all that easy. This was over twenty years ago when the IVF process was relatively experimental. Of course, lots of guys would be willing to participate—"

"But not so many women."

The procedure for harvesting eggs was more complicated than the male side of the fertilization equation. How had Prentice convinced these women to be involved? She tried to imagine how she'd react if approached by a scientist and asked to donate the most personal, most private part of herself.

"Eve? Are you all right?"

"I'm thinking." *Be logical.* If Prentice had asked her to volunteer to be pregnant, she would have certainly refused. Raising a child changed the entire focus of her life and involved a great deal more than mere biology. But giving up an egg? Or two? Or ten? "I would have done it. In the name of science and to help other women who were infertile, there's a more than sixty-six percent chance that I would have said yes."

"Like your biological mother."

Here was evidence: her values were similar to those of the nameless, faceless woman who had donated her egg. Eve wondered what other traits they shared. Had her mother been a scientist? More important, was she also Blake's mother? There had to be a way to calculate the odds.

She remembered an earlier conversation. "There were twenty-four superbabies in the study."

"How do you know that?"

"Vargas told me."

At the mention of Vargas's name, Blake scowled. "Keep in mind that he might also be your brother."

"Whatever." She wasn't attracted to Vargas, certainly not in the same way she was drawn to Blake. "It does seem likely that there were fewer female volunteers—each being given a drug that caused them to produce several eggs per cycle. The question is—how many? Four? Fourteen?"

"Without the documentation, there's no way of knowing."

She hated the uncertainty, hated the possibility that she and Blake could be genetically related. Finally, she'd found a man who rang her chimes, and he might be her brother.

"It can't be," she said emphatically. "We don't look anything alike. Don't have the same coloring. My eyes are blue. Yours are brown."

"That's not proof."

Reaching up, she pushed back the hair on his forehead.

"Ha! You don't have a widow's peak, but I do. That's a dominant characteristic." She grabbed his chin and turned his head. "Oh, no, we both have detached ear lobes."

He shoved her hands away. "Stop groping me."

"I'm not." If he was her brother, groping would be sick. "I need to develop a probability model for you and me utilizing secondary physical traits."

"Face it," he said. "Until we have access to information about our biological parents, we won't know for sure."

"DNA," she said triumphantly. "All we have to do is compare our DNA."

"The testing could take a while."

"I've already had my DNA profiled." She'd volunteered for a study in grad school. "It'll take some digging, but I can get the results. How about you?"

"The army requires that you give blood for DNA testing, and I know my sample has been processed."

He raised his coffee mug to his lips, trying to hide the tension in his mouth. Again, she marveled at how easily she could read his expressions. She knew, without asking, that the processing of his DNA was related to an unfortunate event, probably to get positive identification for a soldier killed in action. "I'm sorry," she said.

"Sarge was a good man. He gave his life to save the rest of the platoon. We were forced into hiding for ten days."

During which time, the army must have compared his remains with the DNA of the other missing soldiers. Her heart ached for Blake's sadness and his sorrow. The empathy she felt was painful, as if they were truly close. As close as a sister?

"We need to get those DNA results," she said. "And we need to move our investigation forward. I don't want to hear any more grumbling about how you always work alone. We're in this together."

"Got it, sis."

"Don't," she snapped. "Don't joke about it."

He finished his coffee and rinsed the cup in the sink. "Where do we start? You said you had a lead."

"Dr. Trevor Latimer." She went to the kitchen table, flipped open the condolence book and ran her finger down the page until she was pointing to the name. "Not only was he at the funeral, but I recognized his name from the clinic where Prentice met me for my supposed examination. Do you know him?"

"We probably shook hands at the funeral. I don't remember."

"He knew your father. And he knows Prentice. I say we start with him. Maybe your father had an address book."

Blake gave a quick nod. "I've got a better idea. Follow me."

She trailed him down the hallway toward his father's office. When she found herself checking out his broad shoulders and tight butt, she groaned and looked away. Sisters do *not* notice if their brothers have cute bottoms.

He opened a door halfway down the hall, and she followed him into his bedroom. As soon as she looked at the queen-size bed with the navy-blue comforter, her imagination flashed an image of Blake sprawled out on that bed. *Wrong!* She turned toward the wall and faced an array of framed photos. The tidy grouping made her think this was his mother's decorating work.

In a group picture of men in army fatigues, Blake stood with his buddies. All were shirtless. She couldn't take her eyes off Blake's muscular chest and six-pack abs. He had an incredible body. *Wrong!*

Standing at the desk, he powered up his laptop. "Let's check out our suspect."

His bedroom was fairly small. Apart from the chair

behind the desk, there was nowhere to sit except for the bed, and she decided against lounging there. She fidgeted. "You said something about sleeping in the same room. That's not going to work for me."

"Not in here," he agreed. "The guest bedroom next door has two single beds."

"Terrific," she muttered. They'd be separated by probably four or five feet of wide-open space. No temptation at all? Ha! "Anything on Latimer?"

He read from the computer screen. "He's an M.D., an OB-GYN who specializes in treating infertility. That explains how he'd know Prentice."

When Latimer allowed Prentice to use the facilities at his clinic, he might just have been doing a favor. "Any indication of how he knew your father?"

"I'm looking at Latimer's photo. He wears glasses. Looks young."

She moved toward the computer so she could see the picture, which meant she was also closer to Blake. Carefully keeping a space between them, she read the biography of Trevor Latimer. "He's twenty-five years old, born in New Mexico."

"Like us. And Vargas."

Latimer had the smarts to be a superbaby. A doctor with his own clinic at age twenty-five had to be a genius. "I guess that answers the question of how he knew your father. He was part of the study."

"We should pay him a visit."

"Now?"

When Blake stood up, his arm accidentally brushed against hers, and they both took a step backward. He checked his G-Shock wristwatch which was typical wear for Special Forces. "It's not even nine o'clock."

It felt much later. This day had been packed with

revelations—emotional highs and lows and everything in between. She knew that from this day forward, her life was changed. "I'm ready if you are."

He strode to his bed, reached under the pillow and pulled out an automatic pistol. "Ready."

Chapter Eight

Blake wasn't drunk, not even close, but he left the driving
to Eve and rode shotgun in the passenger seat of his dad's
station wagon. As she drove, he scanned the streets, looking for any anomaly that might turn into a threat: a person
in a parked car, headlights following them, a loiterer with
a cell phone.

Nothing he saw set off alarm bells.

Eve merged smoothly onto the highway leading toward
downtown Denver. "How am I doing?" she asked.

"Smooth and steady."

"I'm a good driver," she said. "And an excellent
partner."

To tell the truth, he was glad to have her working with
him. During the past several days since he had returned to
town, he'd been butting his head against stone walls. The
homicide detectives and their forensic teams responded
quickly to his questions and had given priority to the au-
topsy so the body could be released for burial. But they'd
been convinced from the start that his dad was the victim
of a burglary gone wrong. Their investigation was cursory
at best.

Likewise, the family attorney wasn't much help. His
focus was on putting his dad's affairs in order.

His aunt Jean had advised him to accept his dad's passing and move on with his life.

Until he hooked up with Eve, his investigation had gone nowhere. Together, they were taking action. It felt good.

He leaned back in the passenger seat and considered Trevor Latimer as a suspect. If his dad was killed to suppress information about the study, there had to be something in those stolen documents that threatened Dr. Latimer. Or maybe the young OB-GYN was a loyal protégé of Prentice, willing to kill to protect his mentor from embarrassing, possible actionable revelations. Why did Latimer come to the funeral? Revisiting the scene of his crime?

In central Denver, Eve parked at the curb outside an impressive two-story, white stucco house with a cupola on top of the red-tiled roof. She gave a low whistle. "Looks like Dr. Latimer has done pretty well for himself."

"Like Vargas," Blake said. "How come I didn't get biological parents with the millionaire gene?"

"Me, neither."

"Does that mean we're kind of alike?"

She punched his arm. "I'm not your sister."

Her voice was angry, frustrated. He could tell that she was a lot more shaken up by their possible genetic relationship than he was. To be sure, a brother and sister shouldn't be hot for each other. He shouldn't be yearning to touch her, shouldn't be turned on by her scent or the way her mouth twisted when she was thinking. But this wasn't the first time in his life that he had to stifle his sexual appetite. He could cope.

Together they proceeded along the curved sidewalk leading to the front door. The meticulous landscaping, groomed flower beds and artistically pruned shrubs were well-lit. A wrought-iron railing marked one edge of the path.

A golden light shone from the left side of the house. Through the polished glass of the bay window, he saw a tall, thin man with glasses playing a violin. The bluesy, mellow tones of "Harlem Nocturne" were audible. A piano accompanied.

Eve paused to listen. "Beautiful."

And sexy. The music made him think of summer nights and sultry, forbidden desires. It made him think of Eve in stilettos and a black silk slip. He blinked to erase that inappropriate and totally unrealistic image. She probably didn't own a pair of high heels.

At the carved, double door, he rang the bell. The music continued as the door was opened by a stocky, balding man in a button-down blue shirt and dress slacks. A five-o'clock shadow darkened his jowls. "May I help you?"

"We're here to see Dr. Latimer. He was at my father's funeral today. I'm Blake Jantzen."

"Yes, I recognize you."

"Were you at the funeral?"

"I'm Dr. Latimer's driver. Please come in. I'll see if he's available."

He and Eve waited in the tiled entryway. The design of the house reminded him of a soft-serve, vanilla ice-cream cone—all rounded edges and curved archways. From where they stood, they could see through the front room to a series of French doors that opened onto a garden, also well-lit. When the music stopped, the resulting silence felt ominous. He thought of Nero fiddling while Rome burned.

Blake unbuttoned his blazer, giving him access to the holster he wore on his hip. He counted the seconds. Latimer was obviously here; they'd seen him through the window. If he refused to meet with them, it could only be because he had something to hide.

The driver returned and beckoned to them. "This way."

The study with the bay window was furnished in earthy southwestern tones. The gracious proportions of the room and the floor-to-ceiling bookcase gave the impression of solidity, as if this home had been here for a hundred years.

The tall, blond man he'd seen through the window tilted his head and looked down his nose through his glasses. He held his violin in his left hand and extended his right. "I'm surprised to see you, Blake. Again, my deepest condolences for your loss."

His linen shirtsleeves had been rolled up to the elbow, revealing thin forearms and long, skeletal fingers. Nonetheless, his grip was strong.

Standing behind a portable keyboard was someone else who had attended the funeral. His name was Peter Gregory. Blake had known him since they were teenagers but hadn't seen him for a couple of years. Peter's style had changed. He wore about four pounds of silver jewelry in rings, cuff bracelets, neck chains, earrings and a nose ring. Everything else was black and tight. His black hair stuck out in spikes. Eyeliner circled his pale gray eyes.

Blake introduced him to Eve. "Peter Gregory. His dad shares an office with mine."

When he bumped fists with Eve, she said, "Your father is a psychiatrist. That must be interesting."

"Not the word I'd use for daddy dearest."

When she shook hands with Latimer, he noticed that the doctor didn't move from where he stood. People came to him, not the other way around. He held on to her hand and leaned closer to her, squinting behind his thick glasses.

His lips thinned in a smile. "Are congratulations in order, Ms. Weathers?"

Eve snatched her hand away. "How did you know?"

"I'm an OB-GYN, specializing in infertility. I've come to recognize the glow that comes when a woman is pregnant."

"Do you know Dr. Edgar Prentice?" she asked.

"Oh, yes. For a long time."

When he reached back and felt the arm of the chair before sitting, Blake understood Latimer's aloof manner. He was visually impaired. That explained the bright lights and the railing by the path.

What Blake didn't readily comprehend was the connection with Lou Gregory's son. The aristocratic Latimer and the leather-clad, obviously antisocial Goth guy were a mismatch. "How do you two know each other?"

"We met at the cemetery," Latimer said. "After we talked, we discovered we were both part of an IVF study that your father did with Prentice."

His dad's funeral had pulled in the superbabies like a magnet. Not an unexpected result. Each of these subjects had communicated with his father once a year for the survey; he had been part of their lives.

"Us, too," Eve said as she pointed to herself and to him. "We were part of the study."

Blake watched both men for their reactions. Peter shrugged as if he couldn't care less, while Latimer seemed mildly interested.

"I must admit," Latimer said, "I never understood the purpose of the study, other than tracking a group of subjects born at about the same time. But I did enjoy my talks with your father. Dr. Ray employed techniques for the treatment of post-traumatic stress disorder to help me cope with my recent disability."

Eve settled at the end of the sofa nearest him. "Were you injured?"

"My, you're direct." He turned his head toward her. "What's your profession? Scientist?"

"Mathematician," she said. "I didn't mean to be pushy about your injury."

"Just curious," he said. "I understand. Three years ago in Indonesia, I was infected by a virus that caused nerve damage and degeneration of my vision. I'm legally blind."

She reached out and touched his hand. "Will you recover?"

"I like to believe there's a possibility."

"Hope is good."

Her smile was bright and friendly. Though Blake wouldn't have chosen such a straightforward approach, he thought she was doing a good job getting Latimer to open up.

Peter Gregory was another story. He'd gone behind his keyboard. His fingers floated above the keys as if playing a silent melody.

The stocky driver stepped into the room. "Can I bring anyone a drink?"

Though Eve looked as if she was going to say yes, Blake quickly refused for both of them.

"Nothing for me," Peter said. "It's time for me to hit the road."

"So soon?" Latimer's disappointment was evident in his voice. "Please come back any time. I very much enjoyed sharing my music with you."

Peter came out from behind the keyboard and approached Latimer. "Before I go, may I? One more time?"

"Of course." Latimer handed over the finely grained rosewood violin. To Eve, he explained, "This rare instrument was crafted by Scolari of Cremona. When Peter and I talked, he couldn't wait to see the Scolari."

With the violin settled under his chin, Peter flexed his ringed fingers and drew the bow across the strings. The resulting sound had a deep, incredible resonance. Peter closed his eyes and played. Each note trembled with distinct clarity. Blake recognized the piece as a concerto his mother had played on the piano, but the music truly came to life on the violin. Peter was brilliant. Like Vargas. And Latimer. It couldn't be coincidence that three of the superbabies were gifted musicians.

As the last notes faded, Eve exhaled a deep, appreciative sigh. "Amazing. You've got to be a professional."

"That's right." He carefully placed the violin on its stand and faced them. "I'm Pyro."

"Wow, I've heard of you," Eve said. "One of the guys I work with is a big fan. You do techno-metal rock, right?"

"I'm not into labels." He sneered. "If I was, I'd call our music post-apocalyptic punk with a metal edge."

"I know one of your songs. 'Eat the Beast.' Right?"

He gave a short laugh as he went back to his keyboard. "It's 'Beat the Beast,' baby."

He slammed out a series of chords and let out an unintelligible wail that set Blake's teeth on edge. Why would somebody who played Mozart like an angel assault the ear drums with this crap? When he made eye contact with Peter/Pyro, he saw a reflection of darkness and rage. "Did you ever play for my dad?"

"Dr. Ray wasn't into my original compositions."

Because he had taste. Of the three superbabies they'd met, Pyro was the most likely to have had more than a superficial relationship with his father. Their families knew each other. "What about your dad? Does he like—"

"We don't talk."

The edge of hostility between them grew wider and

deeper. Blake's instincts told him that Pyro was an enemy.

Eve bounced to her feet. "I like your stuff. If you're playing around here, I'd love to get tickets. For my friend."

"Tomorrow night. At Bowman Hall on Colfax. It's going to be my last show for a while." He started packing up his keyboard. "I'll leave backstage passes at the box office."

"Thanks." She beamed. "It's been great meeting you both. Dr. Latimer, you have a beautiful home."

"Thank you, but this house belongs to my parents. After my father left the military, he established a successful import/export business which he insists on running day to day, even though he's in his seventies."

"What's the name of his business?" Blake asked.

"Latimer and Son." A frown pulled at the corners of his mouth. "His dynastic ambitions were thwarted when I went into medicine. My mother, rest her soul, encouraged me to be a doctor. Specifically, an obstetrician. She called Dr. Prentice a miracle worker. She was forty-four when I was born. She and my father had given up hope of having a child when Prentice approached them."

"They could have adopted," Eve said.

"I agree," he said quickly. "But not my father. He wanted his bloodline to continue."

"So, he was happy when you came along."

"My birth changed his life."

A snapshot of Dr. Latimer's history began to form in Blake's mind. He'd been a late-in-life baby, much like Blake. After his son's birth, his father quit the military and founded a business, something he could leave to his only child.

Latimer cleared his throat. "Though I'm glad to be better acquainted with you both, I can't help wondering why you've come here tonight."

"The study," Pyro grumbled. "That's what this is about."

Blithely ignoring his hostility, Eve said, "Actually, we were trying to reach Dr. Prentice. Do either of you know where we could find him?"

"At his clinic in Aspen," Latimer said.

"He's on vacation," Eve said. "Since you both have the same specialty, I thought you might have some idea where he'd vacation."

He gestured toward the doorway where his driver stood silently. "Randall, would you please find the phone numbers for Dr. Prentice?"

Eve continued to press. "Have you ever consulted with Prentice?"

"Occasionally," he said.

"I suppose that when he's in town, he visits your clinic. Maybe even sees patients there."

"He's used my facilities." Latimer steepled his long, slender fingers. "Frankly, my research has taken a far more experimental direction. Genetics is a vital, aggressive field, and Prentice hasn't kept up with the times."

"Whatever," Pyro said. "I'm outta here."

"Wait." Blake wanted to see their reactions when he told them about the study. "There's something you need to know."

Pyro looked bored, shifting his weight from foot to foot. "Spit it out."

"Dr. Latimer, you asked why my dad would want to monitor the babies born in the study. It's because we shared more than in vitro conception. The embryos were genetically engineered, using the sperm and egg of highly intelligent, physically healthy donors."

Latimer paled. "Are you saying that my mother and father aren't my biological parents?"

"They didn't know," Blake said. "They weren't told."

Pyro threw back his head and laughed. "I knew it. I knew that old fart wasn't really my father."

In contrast, Latimer appeared to be devastated. He sank lower in his chair. "I don't believe you. Dr. Prentice would never do anything so unethical."

Eve moved toward him. "This must be a shock."

He waved her away with an elegant flip of his wrist. "Please leave."

"I'm so sorry." She shot Blake an angry glance. "We should have been careful in the way we told you."

"Leave," Latimer said. "I wish to be alone."

Blake guided her toward the door. Before they left, Randall handed him a note with phone numbers. In a low voice, he asked, "Is it true?"

"Afraid so."

"Dr. Latimer won't be happy." His heavy brows pulled into a scowl. "He's had a rough few years. You should have known him before the illness. He was a different man."

"Randall!" Latimer called from the study.

The stocky driver opened the door and ushered them out.

Pyro dashed outside ahead of them. He danced on the lawn, still laughing. "I'm reborn, man. This is the best day. Ever."

Blake glanced back toward the house. "Not for everyone."

Chapter Nine

Because she hated unquantifiable variables, Eve thought their conversation with Latimer had been unsatisfactory. Though he accused her of being too direct, he'd been far too vague. Was he closely in contact with Prentice? Close enough to kill for him? She tossed the car keys to Blake and slipped into the passenger seat.

Before he started the car, he handed her the note from Randall. "Nothing new here. You already had these phone numbers for Prentice."

"We did learn one important clue."

"What's that?"

"Latimer talked to Prentice today. That's the only way he'd know I'm pregnant."

"What about the glow?"

"Oh, please. That's an old wives' tale."

On the street in front of them, Pyro loaded his keyboard into a van parked under the streetlight. He wouldn't be hard to trace; his vanity license plate proudly repeated his name: PYRO. Turning to face them, he snapped both hands open. A flame exploded from his fingers.

"Wow!" She applauded. "Very cool."

"Lighter fluid," Blake muttered. "Cheap trick."

Pyro bowed before he jumped into the driver's seat and took off.

"He seems awfully happy to have different parents." She was a little bit fascinated by this techno-punk rocker who played classical violin, but she didn't trust him. "Do you think he's faking?"

"Hard to tell. He's a performer."

"I've heard that when a person lies, there are measurable physical reactions. Dilated pupils. Sudden hand gestures. Licking of lips."

"Handy information if you're questioning a suspect in a laboratory," Blake said as he drove to the corner and turned.

"Do you have experience in that field?" As soon as she spoke, she realized her question was obvious. He was Special Forces. "Of course, you've done interrogations."

"Let's just say that I've dealt with my share of informants and rats. When it comes to lying and liars, I usually go with my gut reaction."

"What does your gut tell you?"

"Both these guys have something to hide."

She'd been watching Latimer when Blake had revealed that he was not, in fact, genetically related to the parents who had raised him. Though she hadn't been able to see the doctor's eyes clearly behind his thick glasses, his fingers had tensed. He'd inhaled a quick, sharp gasp. Obvious reactions.

"From what Latimer said about his father," she said, "the genetic truth could create problems."

"Oh, yeah. Old man Latimer sounds like a 'blood is thicker than water' type. He wants an heir, a son to carry on his family name and business." Abruptly, Blake pulled over to the curb. "That's what I call a motive."

"Why are you parking?"

"I want to see what Latimer does next." He opened his car door. "Coming?"

"Are you suggesting that we spy on him?"

"That's the plan."

She hesitated for half a second to consider the ethics of their actions. Spying was sneaky. But they were looking for a murderer, which justified a certain amount of devious behavior. She hopped from the car and followed him as he dashed across the wide lawns in this upscale neighborhood. Though the city streetlights provided clear illumination, the tall trees and ample shrubbery created shadows.

When they rounded the corner, she saw headlights on the street. Blake pulled her close and ducked behind a shrub. He crouched close behind her. She heard his breathing, felt the warmth of his body. The physical attraction she'd managed to put on hold rose up again.

She tried to funnel her thinking in a different direction. "What did you mean when you mentioned motive?"

"Suppose that Dr. Latimer's father found out about the genetics. He'd be ticked off, might even disinherit his son. The good doctor would lose his cushy lifestyle."

His logic made sense to her. "So if Dr. Ray threatened to reveal the information in the study, Latimer had a motive to kill him."

"Yep."

"One thing he's not faking is his blindness," she said. "I noticed a couple of books in Braille on the shelves."

The headlights passed, and Blake guided her closer to Latimer's white stucco mansion. Instead of peeking in the front bay window, they crept around to the side of the house. Blake peeked at the edge of a window and whispered, "He's on the phone. Looks pissed off."

"Can you hear what he's saying?"

"Not really." He leaned closer, nearly pressing his cheek against the glass. "Now, he's talking to Randall. I think he said something about the car."

"Are they going somewhere?"

"That would be my guess," he said. "They left the room."

From far inside the house, she heard a door slam.

"Let's go," Blake said. "We need to follow them."

Abandoning subtlety, they raced across the grassy lawns toward the corner where the vehicle was parked. The short sprint got her blood pumping. When she dove into the passenger seat and closed the door, she felt exhilarated.

"Down!" Blake pushed her forward so her head was on her knees. "There's a car coming out of the alley."

When the headlights passed, she popped up. "Was it them?"

"I saw Randall in the driver's seat." He fired up the engine. "Fasten your seat belt."

As she buckled up, he maneuvered the station wagon around and whipped toward the main road. His driving was pure Indy 500. "You're going too fast. You'll attract attention."

"I need to see which way they turn at the stoplight."

She peered through the windshield. "Is that the car? The one with the rhomboid taillights?"

"If rhomboid means wraparound, yes."

On the main boulevard, she focused on the taillights as Blake dodged through traffic, keeping a distance from the car Randall was driving. When a truck pulled between them, she buzzed down the window and stuck her head out. She still couldn't see the rhomboid lights. "The next time we stop, I can jump out and see where they are."

"Stay in the car."

Their pursuit of the other vehicle was turning out to be fun. Who knew investigating could be such a kick?

When Randall headed northwest, she recognized the

route. "They're going to Dr. Latimer's clinic. I'm sure of it."

"How far is it? Can we get ahead of them?"

"With the way you drive, yes." She glanced up at the street sign and read the number. "Go straight. I'll tell you when to turn."

Using three lanes of traffic as cover, he zipped through a yellow light, leaving Randall behind. "We'll get there first and be out of the car before they arrive."

He parked on the far side of the square three-story building and flung open his door. She leaped from the car and followed him. They hid in the shadows at the edge of the building just as Randall drove toward the front entrance.

Jiggling a set of keys in his hand, Latimer's driver left the car and approached the building.

"Where's Latimer?" she whispered.

"Still in the car."

"How can you tell?"

"Randall left the engine running." Blake leaned his back against the wall. "Latimer has a clear view of the entrance, so we can't follow Randall inside."

"But Latimer's vision isn't good."

"Even if he can't identify us, he'll sure as hell notice two figures breaking into his building."

Two floors above them, office lights went on. She tilted her head back as if she could see through the glass and stone. "Randall is looking for something. Your father's missing documents?"

"I'd like to think you're right, but Latimer's no fool. He wouldn't keep anything incriminating in his office."

She stood beside him. Shoulder to shoulder, but not touching. "Were you really going to break in?"

"Maybe not. There's probably a surveillance camera

pointed at the entrance, and I wouldn't want you to get arrested."

"I could handle it."

She gazed up at his perfect profile, and he smiled down at her. They were well and truly partners. Hard to believe. When she'd gotten out of bed this morning and dressed in black for the funeral, she never dreamed her life would be so radically altered by nightfall. She'd started the day as a solitary mathematician. Now she was pregnant, and she'd met a man who was...someone special.

The lights above them went out.

She peeked around the edge of the building, waiting until Randall emerged. He went to the car and opened the door. Very clearly, she heard him say, "It's safe."

They drove away.

AFTER RETURNING TO HIS father's house, Eve went to the guest bedroom with the matching twin beds and got settled. She shoved her suitcase out of the way in the closet and unzipped the top. Since she'd been at the end of her laundry cycle, her choice in nightwear had been severely limited. Not that she owned any silky lingerie, but this outfit was super geeky: blue flannel pajama bottoms with images of Wonder Woman and an oversize T-shirt in faded red with the Hogwarts coat of arms.

In the adjoining bathroom, she washed her face, brushed her teeth and changed into her dorky nightclothes, telling herself that looking good didn't matter. She didn't want to be desirable. Nothing was going to happen between her and Blake. At least not until after they compared their DNA and knew for sure that they weren't related.

Though there was a desk in the pastel-green bedroom, she took her laptop to bed, where she sat cross-legged in the middle of the green-and-brown plaid bedspread.

Powered up, she began to search for her old friend Hugo, who had used her DNA results for an experimental profile of humans and orangutans. Since she hadn't contacted Hugo in three years, she suspected his old e-mail name—MonkeyMan—was incorrect. Sure enough, her message bounced back in seconds. But she knew his interests—primatology, Indiana Jones movies and saving the rainforest. He wouldn't be hard to locate.

She heard a tap on the door and called out, "Come in."

Like her, Blake had changed into sleep clothes. Even though he was carrying her purse, his army-green T-shirt and black sweatpants looked sexy. She noticed the lower edge of a tattoo peeking out from the sleeve on his left arm.

"All right," she said, "show it to me."

His eyebrows lifted. "What exactly did you want to see?"

She felt herself blushing. "Your tattoo, of course."

He rolled up his sleeve to reveal a winged man. "Icarus," he said. "From the ancient Greek story about the danger of flying too close to the sun. All the men in my platoon got this tat to honor Sarge. His name was Isaacs, and he hated the nickname Icky. Still, I like to think of him flying high."

She'd been ready to give him a hard time about creepy body art, but his tattoo had deep significance—a very valid reason for a tat. "I have one, too."

"Where?"

She pulled down the collar of her Hogwarts T-shirt to show him the one-inch long tattoo. "The symbol of pi. I got it to celebrate my master's degree."

After a quick glance, he looked away as though embarrassed. Him? A great big macho Special Forces guy? Did the top of her left breast intimidate him?

He dropped the purse on her bed. "Check the messages on your cell phone. You had a call from Vargas."

"You looked at my cell phone? I never gave you permission to pry into—"

"Hey, I didn't listen to your messages." He flopped onto the bed beside hers. "Let's hear what the billionaire has to say."

She took out her cell phone, noting that she'd received several calls from the guys at the lab and one from her neighbor. Setting the phone to be on speaker, she played back the Vargas call.

"Hi, Eve. It's David Vargas. I'd like to meet you for lunch tomorrow. One o'clock at the Gilpin Grill in Cherry Creek. This isn't strictly pleasure. I have some business to discuss—an idea that might benefit the research you're doing at Sun Wave."

"Clever," Blake said. "He's trying to hook you with a business proposition."

Or maybe he was actually attracted to her. Was that so hard to believe? "What should I say?"

"Meet him." He rolled onto his back.

"Are you coming with me?"

"Don't tell Vargas that I am. But, yeah. I'm your bodyguard. I go where you go."

First, she called her neighbor and made arrangements for the feral cats. Then, she texted an acceptance to Vargas. The callbacks to coworkers would wait until tomorrow. She looked over at the other bed where he had burrowed under the plaid comforter. Sleeping? Though it was almost midnight, she was wide awake. "Blake?"

"What?"

"When Randall said, 'It's safe,' he might have been talking about security."

"Didn't we already discuss this?"

"Yes, but we were trying to think of an object. Like your father's documents. Or Latimer's DNA test results. A photo. Some kind of proof. What if Randall meant that the whole office was safe."

"Tomorrow. We'll think about it tomorrow."

As she gazed at his lumpy form, she found herself wishing he'd stay up and talk to her, maybe even give her a good-night kiss. Even if it was wrong? Even if he was her brother? With a renewed sense of purpose, she returned to her computer search.

After a few minutes, he growled, "When are you going to turn off the light?"

"As soon as I locate MonkeyMan."

"Is that a porno site or your boyfriend?"

"Neither. MonkeyMan was the e-mail name for Hugo Resnick, a primatologist. He's the guy who did my DNA. Shouldn't you be looking for your own DNA results?"

"Tomorrow, we're going to a clinic at Fitzsimons," he said. "I figure General Walsh will be able to access my results a lot easier than I can."

"Why Fitzsimons? I thought the veteran hospital was closed."

"My dad worked there part-time at the PTSD clinic. It's a place he might have kept copies of his documents. Plus, I need equipment to continue with this investigation."

"Like what?"

"Another weapon, ammo, bugging devices, infrared goggles and a vehicle. My dad's old station wagon is fine for trips to the grocery store. But I need a car with more horses."

He was such a typical male. "It's all about the hard-ware."

"You guessed it."

Within fifteen minutes, she'd located Hugo the Mon-keyMan and sent him an e-mail. Hopefully, he wasn't in Borneo doing research. With luck, she'd have a reply from him tomorrow.

She turned off the bedside lamp and got under the covers. "Good night, Blake."

"Night."

She'd barely gotten settled when she heard a loud buzz-ing noise. The house alarm had been activated.

Chapter Ten

At the sound of the alarm, Blake was awake. Alert. Ready.

The Sig Sauer that had been on the bedside table was in his hand. Safety off, he aimed two-handed at the closed bedroom door. He reversed position, pointed the barrel at the thin light filtering through the plaid curtains on the windows. No immediate threat was visible.

He scissored his legs free from the comforter, leaped across the narrow space between the twin beds and covered Eve with his body. He'd wanted to touch her. But not like this, damn it.

No time to explain. He pulled her off the bed.

In a few steps, they were inside the adjoining bathroom where the only window was high off the floor. Unfortunately, there wasn't a bathtub where she could take cover.

He felt her standing close behind him. No whimpering. No complaining. Like a good soldier, she was waiting for him to tell her what to do. *A damn good question.*

They could hunker down and wait for the security company to respond in ten, maybe fifteen minutes. With the bathroom door ajar and his Sig Sauer aimed at the closed door leading into the bedroom, Blake was confident that he could hold off the threat until help arrived, but it went against his grain to sit back and wait. He wanted to nab this son of a bitch.

As if she'd read his mind, Eve said, "You want to go after him."

"I can't leave you unguarded."

"They won't hurt me." She spoke loudly enough to be heard over the alarm. "The only reason they're after me is the baby. They want to monitor my pregnancy, make sure I don't give the baby up for adoption."

"Your logic is solid." *As always.*

"You're the one in danger, Blake."

She was right. Her baby was the prize, and he fell into the category of collateral damage. They'd shoot him to reach her, but he was willing to take that chance.

From the instant he heard the alarm until now couldn't have been more than four minutes. He eased open the bathroom door and took a step. "Stay here."

"While you risk your life?" She latched on to his arm, preventing him from leaving. "No."

He peered through the dim light from the window at her upturned face. He could have given her a long-winded rationale, citing his experience and the need for action, could have told her that victory never went to the faint-hearted. But only one fact was important. "They killed my father."

She winced. Her hand dropped from his arm. "Be careful."

He appreciated her sensibility. She'd been raised on military bases and knew what it meant to be a warrior.

He slipped through the bathroom door. The most likely place for an ambush was the hallway outside the bedroom door. He had to move fast. Stay low.

Opening the bedroom door, he poked his head into the hallway and withdrew. The wood on the doorframe splintered, but he heard nothing but the blaring alarm. The shooter must have been using a silencer.

His instincts and training told him to attack. Dive into the hallway and roll, come up with his gun blazing.

He felt Eve's touch on his shoulder. What the hell? She should have stayed in the bathroom.

"The window," she said. "You can catch up to him outside when he tries to escape."

Smart. "Open the window and take a look. If you don't see anybody, jump out."

While she did as he said, he fired into the hallway, engaging the shooter.

When he saw Eve slide through the window, he ran across the bedroom and followed. His chest scraped against the narrow casement frame, but he was outside in a moment.

He could already hear the approaching sirens. The shooter inside the house would be making his escape. From the front or the back? He scanned the cars parked on the cul-de-sac.

Beside him, Eve said, "I don't see the SUV that was outside my house."

The back of his father's house opened onto a yard with a fence. Beyond was a strip of forest with pines and cottonwoods that separated this property from the neighboring development. If Blake had broken into this house, he would have chosen that route.

He looked down at Eve. "I can't drag you into the forest. Too risky."

"The sirens are close. As soon as they're here—"

"That's when I'll go."

The streetlight slanted a dramatic shadow across her

face. She reached up and placed her hand on his cheek. "Please don't get yourself killed."

"I never do."

She kissed him. Her lips pressed hard against his, taking his breath away. It felt too good to be wrong.

When the security vehicle came into sight, she ran toward it. He took off in the opposite direction, circling the house. The porch light over the back door was off, and the lights from the street didn't reach this far.

He crept through the moonlight, hiding in shadow and cursing himself for being barefoot. He kept in constant motion, knowing that to stand in one place meant he'd be an easy target. He employed every caution but felt no fear. This was his element. He'd been trained in armed pursuit and capture.

At the fence, he peered into the trees. A night wind rustled the branches. The alarm and the noise from the security team arriving at the front of the house masked the sounds of the intruder retreating.

To his far left, he saw movement. He squeezed off a couple of shots and ducked. He saw the flash of gunfire. The intruder had gone this way.

He jumped the fence and ran toward the place where he'd seen gunfire, dodging behind trees and taking shots when he could. Though he hadn't been counting, he knew he was almost out of bullets.

The pine needles, twigs and cones tore at the soles of his feet, but he was narrowing the gap, closing in on his quarry. A burst of loud gunfire told him that the man with the silencer had been joined by another shooter.

There were at least two of them and one of him. They were armed. He was almost out of ammo. And barefoot.

But he had backup. He heard the security guards rushing into the backyard behind him.

Firing his last bullets, Blake charged forward.

He emerged from the trees onto a paved street with modern, two-story houses and tidy lawns.

The taillights of an SUV raced away. From this distance, he couldn't tell if it was the same vehicle he'd seen at Eve's house in Boulder.

They turned the corner and were gone.

AFTER THE SECURITY company personnel repaired the lock on the back door and the uniformed police officers left, Blake sat across the kitchen table from the homicide detective who had investigated his father's murder. Detective Joseph Gable propped his chin in his hand as though his neck was too tired to hold up his head. His tan suit was rumpled and had a grease stain on the left lapel. His eyelids drooped. The worry lines across his forehead had deepened to furrows. It was almost two o'clock in the morning. Homicide was a rough beat.

Eve placed two mugs on the table: coffee for Detective Gable and some kind of herbal tea for him. She'd made a fuss over the scratches on his feet. Even though none of his injuries were deep enough to require stitches, she'd cleaned his feet, applied antiseptic and bandages. He didn't need pampering but didn't mind having her play nurse.

She spoke to the detective. "Would you like anything to eat? I can zap some leftovers."

"I'd like some answers." He turned toward Blake. "Where did you get the Sig?"

"General Stephen Walsh," he replied. "After Eve was attacked at her house, I though I might need firepower."

"Do you have other weapons?"

Blake didn't think the homicide detective would be

amused by his display of knife skills or any reference to the fact that he knew thirty-seven ways of killing a man with his bare hands. "I'll be seeing the general tomorrow, after which I expect to be fully armed."

"And dangerous," the detective said. "It's not your job to go after the bad guys. That little shoot-out of yours could have resulted in tragedy."

Eve stepped up to defend him. "We were attacked. Not the other way around."

The detective held up his hand to forestall further comment. "Tell me what you know. I'll take it from here."

As far as Blake was concerned, the police had already had their chance to investigate, and they had failed. He wasn't about to stand down. "Did you find evidence at Eve's house?"

"We got fingerprints. Yours. Eve's, of course. And—"

"Wait a minute," she interrupted. "I didn't give you my fingerprints. Why am I on file?"

Blake grinned. "Something you're not telling me? Are you in ViCAP? Or CODIS?"

"Explain what those letters stand for, and I'll tell you."

"Violent Criminal Apprehension Program is a databank that includes fingerprints. CODIS stands for Combined DNA Index System."

"A list of DNA for criminals," she said thoughtfully.

"It was started to track sex offenders," Gable said, "but it's a much wider scope. Don't worry, you're not in either of those databases. We had a match for your prints because of your work at Sun Wave, handling government contracts in sensitive locations."

"Any other prints at my house?"

"Two other people you work with." His bloodshot

eyes glared in her direction. "We found no sign of a break-in."

"Which I already explained," she said. "I was feeding the alley cats and left the door open. It wasn't smart, but I really didn't expect to be attacked."

"Can you tell me why these guys came after you? And how do they connect to the murder of Ray Jantzen?"

She leaned against the counter. Though she was still wearing her Wonder Woman pajama bottoms, she'd covered her Harry Potter T-shirt with a gray hoodie. With her face washed clean of makeup and her blond hair tousled, she looked younger than twenty-five. "I'm sure Blake has already mentioned the Prentice-Jantzen study."

The detective nodded. "Go on."

"Well, that's the connection," she said. "Have you spoken to Dr. Prentice? What did he tell you?"

"Why do you think he's after you?"

Blake suppressed a grin. Answering a question with another question might throw off the average witness, but Gable didn't know Eve. She had a mathematician's logic and focus.

"Ask Dr. Prentice," she said. "You need to look at his phone records to see who he's contacted, and you should check his bank accounts for large deposits to known criminals. Like hitmen."

"Give me a reason," the detective said. "And I'll get a warrant."

Blake saw the reluctance in her eyes. She didn't want to explain the strange circumstances of her pregnancy, and he didn't blame her. Not only was her story unbelievable, but it violated her privacy.

"Believe me," she said. "If there was anything I could say to help you find the murderer, I'd tell you in a heartbeat."

"I'm listening," he said. "Start at the beginning. What happened at the funeral?"

She shook her head and shrugged.

Detective Gable sipped his coffee, licked his lips and waited for them to speak—standard cop procedure for getting witnesses and suspects to open up.

Blake wasn't interested in wasting time with a stare-down. "Here's the deal. If we discover information you can act on, we'll be in touch."

"I advise against pursuing your own investigation."

"There's no law against asking questions." He held his mug to his lips and inhaled the sweet, minty fragrance. The tea didn't live up to the aroma; it tasted like tree bark.

"I know your reputation, Blake. You're Special Forces. You've got dozens of citations for valor and two Purple Hearts. You're a hero, a man of action. But this is suburban Denver, and we're not at war."

His father had been murdered. He couldn't think of a more compelling reason for him to use his Special Forces training.

"I'm warning you," the detective continued. "No violence. Don't go Rambo on me."

"I understand."

The detective took a final sip of coffee and stood. "You should be safe tonight. The security company left a car and two guards out front."

A service that Blake was paying extra for. He didn't begrudge the money. It was worth it to get a good night's sleep. "We'll be fine."

Detective Gable looked toward Eve. "I can't offer you protection in a safe house, but I would strongly advise you to leave town until this is over."

She nodded. "I appreciate your concern."

On this point, Blake agreed with Detective Gable.

Though he valued Eve's intelligence and enthusiasm, he didn't want to put her in danger.

After he showed the detective to the door and reset the alarm, he turned toward her. "Gable is right."

"About what?"

He hobbled down the hallway. "You should leave town."

In the guest bedroom, he stretched out on the twin bed nearest the door. As soon as he was prone, his injuries caught up with him. The soles of his feet prickled. The scrape on his rib cage where he'd gone through the narrow casement window ached. Running through the forest, he'd gotten a couple of other scratches on his arm. No big deal. Nothing serious. Leaning back against the pillows, he pulled up the covers.

To his surprise, she sat on the edge of the bed beside him, closer than necessary.

"I already considered going somewhere else," she said. "It's not feasible. For the next seven months while I'm pregnant, I'm in jeopardy. And what happens after I give birth? Prentice might come after my child. I can't spend the rest of my life on the run."

The lamplight shone on her cheekbones and chin. He studied her face—her wide, expressive mouth and the cute little bump on her nose. Messy wisps of wheat-blond hair fell across her rosy cheeks. Her lightly tanned complexion highlighted the startling blue of her eyes. All together, she was a fine-looking woman.

"Latimer was right," he said. "You're glowing."

"That's an old wives' tale. Not grounded in science."

He took her hand, laced his fingers with hers. Sister or not, he wanted to kiss her. "You're beautiful, Eve. Golden and warm."

She gave a tug on his hand but didn't pull away. "There's something about me that you should know."

"You can tell me anything."

She turned her head away as though she couldn't bear to look him in the eye. "I'm a virgin."

Oh, hell.

Chapter Eleven

The next morning at Fitzsimons, Eve fidgeted in an uncomfortable chair along the wall in General Walsh's outer office. Her gaze went to a clock on the secretary's desk, watching as the minutes ticked by. She crossed her legs and swung her ankle in tight circles.

"Nervous?" Blake asked.

"I'm fine."

After last night when she'd told him she was a virgin, he'd been more cautious around her, treating her like a fragile piece of glass. But she'd wanted him to know because they kept bumping into each other...with their lips. It seemed impossible to avoid his embrace. Inevitable that they would soon make love.

All night long, she'd dreamed of him. On some level, she'd known that she wasn't actually on a tropical beach with palm trees and a tranquil azure sea. She hadn't really been watching Blake rise from the waves, shake the water from his hair and come toward her. In dreams, her senses had been fooled. She had smelled the salty tang of the surf. Her toes had dug into warm sand. When dream Blake had yanked her into his arms, her lips had tingled and she had tasted his kisses. With her willing hands, she had sculpted his taut biceps, his chest, his abdomen and his thighs. The springy black hair on his chest had tickled her nose as she had trailed kisses down to his belly button.

Her subconscious mind had been sending her a message, telling her loud and clear that Blake was the man she'd been waiting for. She was meant to be with him. Finally, to make love. No longer to be a virgin.

Sitting next to him in this bland office was pure torture. She folded her arms below her breasts to avoid accidentally touching him. When she suddenly gasped, she realized that she hadn't been breathing. To keep from inhaling his scent?

If the general's civilian secretary hadn't been sitting behind her desk and tapping away on her computer, Eve might have given in to her desires and thrown herself on Blake.

"What's wrong?" he asked.

"Nothing," she lied.

"Worried about your lunch with Vargas?"

That thought hadn't crossed her mind. "Maybe I'm a little bit tense."

"Yeah," he said. "Your arms are wrapped tight. Looks like you're wearing an invisible straitjacket."

"You think I'm crazy?"

"A little bit."

She turned her head and dared to look at him. He wasn't wearing camouflage battle fatigues but might as well have been. His cargo pants covered his ankle holster, and she was pretty sure he had other weapons stashed in the pockets. A white T-shirt molded to his chest, and his loose, untucked, black-and-gray patterned shirt hid the knife sheath on his belt.

Her gaze lifted to his perfect face and sank into his dark, chocolate eyes. Purely delicious! Did it really matter if their DNA matched?

She looked away. They'd find out soon. This morning, before she had brushed her teeth or took a shower, she'd powered up her computer to see if MonkeyMan had responded. There was his e-mail with her DNA profile attached. All they needed now was Blake's record.

When the general opened the door to his office, she bounded to her feet so abruptly that she almost stumbled. "Good morning, sir."

"No need for formality." He gestured to his casual slacks and collared golf shirt with a Torrey Pines logo. "Today, I'm just another old duffer. Do either of you golf?"

"Not for a while," Blake said as he shook the white-haired man's hand. "There's a hell of a fine course in Dubai, but most of the Middle East is a giant sand trap."

"Your dad was lousy off the tee but made up for it on the greens. He could sink a sixty-foot putt. No sweat. He used to say that golf was half skill and half psychology."

"And what do you say?" Blake asked.

"It's all about the objective. Get the ball in the hole."

Their small talk was driving Eve crazy. She understood that a certain amount of chat was needed to build trust, and men liked to bond over sports, but she was burning with anxiety. "Speaking of objectives," she said. "Were you able to access Blake's DNA records?"

While the general conferred with his secretary, Blake nudged her shoulder. "Calm down."

Don't tell me to calm down, Mr. Perfect. Dream Blake would have understood her urgency. He would have been as desperate as she was to get those records.

"Not yet," the general said. "My request has been initiated. It'll take a while to get results."

She forced a smile. "Would it help if you said it was a matter of life and death?"

"Not at all, kiddo. This is the army."

"In the meantime," Blake said, "I'd like to see the clinic where my dad worked."

"Sure thing."

The general escorted them into the hallway and down the corridor. As soon as they stepped outside, he said, "I put together the equipment you requested, Blake. And I managed to wrangle up a vehicle worthy of a superspy."

"Thank you, sir."

The general paused, looked up at the blue Colorado sky and ran his hand over his close-cropped white hair. "I promised not to ask questions. To tell the truth, I don't really want to know what you're up to. But I'm not a complete lamebrain."

"No, sir," Blake said.

"Here's what I think. You don't believe the police theory that your father was killed by a burglar. You think his murder was premeditated, and you're going after the man who did it." The general shot him a glare. "Don't answer that."

Eve watched as Blake listened without moving a muscle. Though she'd spent most of her childhood on and around army bases, she'd never been this close to a mission getting under way. Her dad had never shared the details of his assignments with her or Mom, and she hadn't considered his clerical work as an information analyst to be very interesting. Certainly not dangerous.

Now she had to wonder if he'd been privy to the details of espionage. Not all the heroes in the military were Special Forces like Blake.

"I have one concern," the general said. "If you discover that your father was killed by a veteran, leave his punishment to me."

"Yes, sir," Blake said.

She really didn't think Dr. Ray had been killed by one

of his veteran patients, unless one of those men was connected to the Prentice-Jantzen study. She asked, "General, how much do you know about Dr. Edgar Prentice?"

His steely blue eyes connected with hers. His face was expressionless; she couldn't tell if her question had irritated him or aroused his curiosity.

He said, "I know Prentice worked with Blake's dad."

"Twenty-six years ago," she said, "the army funded a study for Prentice and Dr. Ray. On in vitro fertilization."

"Babies aren't my field of expertise. My wife thinks I volunteered for overseas duty to avoid changing diapers."

"How many children do you have?" she asked.

"Five. All girls." A warm grin cracked his stony façade. "And I have three grandbabies. Two boys and another beautiful baby girl."

He started walking again, and she fell into step. Their conversation had given her something to think about other than her outrageously inappropriate lust, and she was glad to find that her brain was capable of normal functioning.

Dr. Ray shared space in a small office with four desks. The only person in the room was a slight, thin man with wire-framed glasses. Though his identification badge identified him as Dr. Puller, he seemed too young to be a counselor. Another superbaby?

Dr. Puller was quick to shake Blake's hand and offer his condolences. "We already packed up your father's belongings," he said. "I thought Connie, our unit secretary, delivered them to your house."

"You're correct," Blake said. "She also delivered a pecan pie, and I owe her a thank-you."

The thin man adjusted his glasses. "Was there something else?"

"A list of his patients," Blake said.

FREE Merchandise is 'in the Cards' for you!

Dear Reader,

We're giving away FREE MERCHANDISE!

Seriously, we'd like to reward you for reading this novel by giving you **FREE MERCHANDISE** worth over **$20**. And no purchase is necessary!

You see the Jack of Hearts sticker above? Paste that sticker in the box on the Free Merchandise Voucher inside. Return the Voucher promptly...and we'll send you valuable Free Merchandise!

Thanks again for reading one of our novels—and enjoy your Free Merchandise with our compliments!

Pam Powers

Pam Powers

P.S. Look inside to see what Free Merchandise is **"in the cards"** for you!

(H-H-08/10)

W

e'd like to send you two free books to introduce you to the Harlequin Intrigue® series. These books are worth over $10, but they are yours to keep absolutely FREE! We'll even send you 2 wonderful surprise gifts. You can't lose!

REMEMBER: Your Free Merchandise, consisting of **2 Free Books** and **2 Free Gifts**, is worth over $20.00! No purchase is necessary, so please send for your Free Merchandise today.

YOUR FREE MERCHANDISE INCLUDES...

2 FREE Harlequin Intrigue® Books
AND 2 FREE Mystery Gifts

FREE MERCHANDISE VOUCHER

2 FREE BOOKS and **2 FREE GIFTS**

Please send my Free Merchandise, consisting of
2 Free Books and **2 Free Mystery Gifts**.
I understand that I am under no obligation to buy
anything, as explained on the back of this card.

*About how many NEW paperback fiction books
have you purchased in the past 3 months?*

❑ 0-2   ❑ 3-6   ❑ 7 or more
E7N6   E7PJ   E7PU

❑ I prefer the regular-print edition   ❑ I prefer the larger-print edition
182/382 HDL   **199/399 HDL**

Please Print

FIRST NAME

LAST NAME

ADDRESS

APT.#   CITY

STATE/PROV.   ZIP/POSTAL CODE

Offer limited to one per household and not valid to current subscribers of Harlequin Intrigue® books.
Your Privacy—Harlequin Books is committed to protecting your privacy. Our Privacy Policy is available online at
www.ReaderService.com or upon request from the Reader Service. From time to time we make our lists of
customers available to reputable third parties who may have a product or service of interest to you. If you would
prefer for us not to share your name and address, please check here ❑ **Help us get it right**—We strive for
accurate, respectful and relevant communications. To clarify or modify your communication preferences, visit us at
www.ReaderService.com/consumerschoice.

NO PURCHASE NECESSARY!

◄ Detach card and mail today. No stamp needed. ▼

© 2010 HARLEQUIN ENTERPRISES LIMITED. ® and ™ are trademarks owned
and used by the trademark owner and/or its licensee. Printed in the U.S.A.

(H1-08/10)

The Reader Service - Here's how it works:

Accepting your 2 free books and 2 free mystery gifts (gifts valued at approximately $10.00) places you under no obligation to buy anything. You may keep the books and gifts and return the shipping statement marked "cancel." If you do not cancel, about a month later we'll send you 6 additional books and bill you just $4.24 each for the regular-print edition or $4.99 each for the larger-print edition in the U.S. or $4.99 each for the regular-print edition or $5.74 each for the larger-print edition in Canada. That's a savings of at least 15% off the cover price. It's quite a bargain! Shipping and handling is just 50¢ per book.* You may cancel at any time, but if you choose to continue, every month we'll send you 6 more books, which you may either purchase at the discount price or return to us and cancel your subscription.

*Terms and prices subject to change without notice. Prices do not include applicable taxes. Sales tax applicable in N.Y. Canadian residents will be charged applicable provincial taxes and GST. Offer not valid in Quebec. All orders subject to approval. Books received may not be as shown. Credit or debit balances in a customer's account(s) may be offset by any other outstanding balance owed by or to the customer. Please allow 4 to 6 weeks for delivery. Offer available while quantities last.

▲ If offer card is missing write to: The Reader Service, P.O. Box 1867, Buffalo, NY 14240-1867 or visit www.ReaderService.com ▲

BUSINESS REPLY MAIL

FIRST-CLASS MAIL   PERMIT NO. 717   BUFFALO, NY

POSTAGE WILL BE PAID BY ADDRESSEE

THE READER SERVICE

PO BOX 1867

BUFFALO NY 14240-9952

NO POSTAGE
NECESSARY
IF MAILED
IN THE
UNITED STATES

"Those files are confidential. But Connie could check the records if you know who you're looking for. I don't think Dr. Ray was seeing anyone outside his regular group sessions. He only worked here one afternoon a week."

Eve asked, "Did you ever sit in on his groups?"

"As often as I could. Dr. Ray brought more than skill to his sessions. A wisdom." He shoved his hands into the pockets of his sweater vest. "I learned by observing him."

His obvious respect for Dr. Ray made her think of the superbabies again. "Dr. Puller, how old are you?"

"Thirty-two."

"You look younger," she said.

"I know." He gave a sheepish grin. "That's why I wear the glasses. My wife says they make me look mature."

She was relieved to know that he wasn't one of the subjects of the study. They already had too many suspicious people to keep track of.

"We're looking for a specific individual," she said. "He might have been one of Dr. Ray's patients. He'd be in his mid-twenties, born in New Mexico. We can't give you a physical description, but he's highly intelligent, gifted."

Puller thought for a moment and shook his head. "Sorry. No one comes to mind."

He took them to the main reception area and introduced them to Connie, who was clearly the brains of this particular unit. While Blake arranged for the secretary to send his father's patient list to his computer, Eve considered the possibility that Dr. Ray had been murdered by a patient.

She didn't have training in psychology, but it seemed logical that a murderer would have an abnormal personality and would, therefore, be seeking psychiatric help.

But Blake's father hadn't been attacked in a fit of homicidal rage. The crime had been premeditated; his records had been stolen. The murderer wanted to suppress the information in those files—a secret that was important enough to kill for.

BLAKE COULDN'T HAVE ASKED for a better vehicle.

In the officer's parking lot, General Walsh glided his hand along the sleek lines of a midnight-blue Mercedes Benz sedan as he detailed the specifications. "She's fully loaded with a V-8 engine and heavy-duty shocks. There's a self-contained, untraceable GPS system and satellite phone. A steel-reinforced frame with an armored roof, floor and side panels. Bulletproof glass, of course, and a ballistic, self-sealing gas tank. You can drive this baby through a war zone and come out the other side without a scratch."

The armored Mercedes was one hell of an upgrade from his dad's serviceable, old station wagon. Blake approached the car with reverence. "I think I'm in love."

"She's a couple years old," the general said, "but still a beauty."

Eve asked, "How many miles per gallon?"

"Irrelevant," Blake said.

"You know I drive a hybrid, and I work at a company developing solar energy systems. It's important to be green."

Not taking his eyes off the Mercedes, he replied, "Would you throw out the Mona Lisa because the paint wasn't water soluble?"

"Your argument is illogical," she said. "You're justifying a questionable ecological decision based on aesthetics."

"You're saying that we should all drive ugly cars."

"If it saves the planet, yes. There should never be a rationale for wasting our precious resources."

He threw out an example he knew she'd understand.

"Like all those resources wasted on the Hubble telescope? Do we really need a better photo of the Horse Nebula?"

"Oh." She went silent.

The general circled around to the trunk and popped it open. "Back here, I stashed the equipment you requested."

Blake checked out the extra guns, ammo, surveillance devices and infrared goggles—all useful tools that would help in investigating. But the Mercedes? It was beyond anything he ever expected. "I don't know how to thank you, sir."

"Your father was a good man. He helped a lot of soldiers. Now, it's my turn to help you."

"Excuse me." Eve popped up beside him. "What is this sort of vehicle used for?"

"Secure protection. A couple of years ago, the Democratic National Convention was held in Denver. There were a lot of high-ranking individuals in town—men and women who were targets for terrorists."

"And you used this vehicle to drive them around."

"We had a whole fleet. This one, we kept." He clapped Blake on the shoulder. "Do the right thing."

Blake was so excited to get behind the wheel that he barely noticed Eve sliding into the passenger seat. He ogled the dashboard. There were as many dials as a cockpit but tastefully displayed in Mercedes Benz style.

When he turned the key in the ignition, the Mercedes hummed at a perfect pitch. Grinning like a lunatic, he glanced at Eve. "You might want to buckle up."

"Why? Is this gas-guzzler going to sprout wings and fly?"

"I wouldn't be surprised."

Driving from the parking lot was like riding on a swift and powerful wind. The smooth leather seats cushioned his butt. The steering handled like a dream. He wanted to take this baby out on the open road. For the first time since he was told of his father's murder, he felt something akin to pure joy.

"Well?" she asked. "Does the car live up to your expectations?"

"She's amazing." He glided to a stop at a light and turned his head toward her. "You look good in a Mercedes."

"Uh-huh. You'd think a brain-sucking zombie looked good in this car."

"I mean it." Nestled in fawn-colored leather, her T-shirt and denim jacket could pass for casual elegance. Her tousled blond hair almost appeared to have style. Most important, she was relaxed. The nervous intensity that plagued her this morning was gone.

When he turned right, she looked up. "This isn't the most direct route to downtown."

"I'm taking the highway," he said. "Because I feel the need."

"The need for speed," she completed the quote. "*Top Gun.* My dad loves that movie."

"Aviators can be a pain in the butt. But they are cool."

She picked up the satellite phone. "I should try calling Prentice on this phone. He wouldn't recognize the number."

"Give it a shot."

She plugged in the number and waited for an answer. "He's not answering."

"Right," he mumbled. "That would be too easy."

"Tell me about the doodads in the trunk."

"High-tech surveillance equipment and weaponry. You're going to like this stuff."

"I'm not interested in guns, Blake. I'd rather have you show me how to defend myself without killing anybody."

Avoiding serious harm to your opponent ran counter to his training. Not that he always fought to the death. But he never held back, no matter what the consequences.

Chapter Twelve

Eve had to admit that the tiny communication device fitted into her ear was a very cool gadget. She heard Blake clearly, even though he'd taken a position down the block from the restaurant where she was supposed to meet David Vargas.

In addition, she wore a microphone pin so Blake could hear what she said. The secret communication made her feel like a superspy. As she entered the Gilpin Grill in Cherry Creek North, she whispered, "I'm going inside."

In her ear, Blake responded, "I know. I can see you. You don't have to tell me everything."

At the door, she was met by a host who whisked her to the leather-padded booth where Vargas awaited. He slid out from behind the table and greeted her with a kiss on both cheeks, which was not the way she usually said hello. Her typical lunch with the Sun Wave crew tended to be pizza or fast food. Not linen tablecloths and heavy silverware. Though many of the restaurant patrons, including Vargas, wore suits, she didn't feel out of place in her denim jacket. This was casual Colorado where millionaires sometimes dressed in beat-up jeans and scruffy boots.

Vargas loosened his necktie, pulled it off and stuffed it into his pocket. "Excuse the corporate uniform. I had a meeting with attorneys this morning."

"Tell me about your business."

"Investments and properties, cashing in and cashing out. Not all that interesting."

He gave her a warm, somehow charismatic smile. His features weren't as perfectly symmetrical as Blake's. His wide-spaced eyes and narrow chin made his face into an inverted triangle, like a cat. The streak of white in his black hair also seemed animalistic.

She noticed his widow's peak—a genetic trait that she shared. Smiling back at him, she said, "It sounds like you work with numbers. That's my field."

"Right. You're a math genius."

"I wouldn't say genius."

"Don't be modest." He signaled to the waitress. "I looked you up. You're well-respected in your field."

She ordered water and checked out the pricey menu. While Vargas discussed wine with the waitress, she heard Blake in her ear. "Get him to talk about the study. He's known for years about his genetic parents."

Having him inside her head was disconcerting. He'd already penetrated her imagination. Images of his face, his arms, his chest and all the other parts played on a continuous loop.

Vargas leaned toward her. "Are you sure you don't want to sample the wine?"

He wouldn't be asking if he knew she was pregnant, which seemed to indicate that he wasn't aware of her condition. On the other hand, he might be testing her. "Water's fine. And I think I'll have the free-range chicken salad."

"I recommend the hamburger. It's Kobe beef." He pulled on his earlobe—a detached earlobe like hers and Blake's.

"Chicken's fine." As far as she was concerned, the time

for small talk was over. "Do you think we're genetically related? You know, brother and sister?"

"You like to get right to the meat," he said.

"Even if it's not Kobe beef."

His voice lowered to a confidential tone. "In the study, Dr. Prentice had a limited number of subjects to use as sperm and egg donors."

He ran through the same logic that she and Blake had already figured out. She asked, "When you found out about the study, did you try to find your genetic parents?"

"Neither Dr. Ray nor Prentice would share that information. Their volunteers were promised that their identities would never be known. Safeguards were taken."

Those volunteers probably never knew what happened after their initial contact with Prentice. Twenty-six years ago, the world was a very different place, with limited Internet access and information sharing. Less technology meant more privacy. More secrets.

In her ear, Blake said, "How does he know safeguards were taken? He's holding something back."

She should have caught that slip from Vargas. "How do you know? About the safeguards?"

His gray eyes widened slightly—only a millimeter, but it was enough to tell her that he was aware that he'd taken a misstep. "Numerical codes were used instead of names."

"And you know this because…"

"I've seen the records."

"You hacked into Prentice's computer files," she said. An excellent idea. "What did you find?"

"There were no names," he said. "Not for the donors and not for the babies. Each individual was assigned a random number. After I had my own DNA run, I could compare. My biological parents are 73 and 15."

The waitress brought his wine to the table, and he went

through the ritual of swirling, sniffing and tasting. His attitude betrayed no sign of nervousness. He seemed to be in absolute control, leading her toward whatever conclusion suited his purposes.

She knew that his hacked data would provide a great more information than random numbers. Having Prentice's files was how Vargas knew there were twenty-four babies. The DNA profiles would indicate gender, and he'd told her that there were only two females. Therefore, he had a fifty percent chance of knowing her relationship to him.

After the waitress left with their order, she rephrased her initial question. "Am I your sister?"

"Half sister." He raised his wineglass to her in a toast. "We share the same mother."

Apparently, she'd misread him from the start. Vargas hadn't been flirting with her. He'd been…establishing a brotherly connection? Somehow, that didn't seem right.

Family was important to her. And by family, she meant the mother and father who had raised her, the grandparents who had spoiled her, the aunts and uncles and cousins who had exchanged birthday cards. Vargas was nothing to her. And yet, he was genetically closer to her than any of those other people.

In her ear, Blake said, "I'll be damned."

"Just what I was thinking," she responded.

"What?" Vargas asked.

"Nothing." She pulled her thoughts together. "Knowing that you're my half brother is disconcerting. It shouldn't make a difference. Our relationship is nothing more than biology."

"I feel something, too. When I saw you at the funeral and figured out who you were, I felt…" He rested his hand on his heart. "An inner warmth. I was happy that I'd found you."

"Wait a minute, how do you know it's me? The other female in the study could be the other woman."

"You both have the same mother. Different fathers, though."

Which meant that Eve had a half sister. If she hadn't been pregnant, she would have drained his wineglass and asked for more. A gallon more. "Where is she?"

"I don't know her name," he said. "The parents who raised us were all in the military, which meant they moved around a lot. And women are harder to trace than men. They get married and change their names."

"Have you located other men who were in the study?"

"I guessed about Blake. And there were a couple of guys at the funeral. Dr. Trevor Latimer?"

In her ear, Blake said, "Don't confirm."

She knew that. *Loose lips sink ships.* "What made you think he was one of us?"

"He's our age and already an OB-GYN with a thriving practice, which indicates high intelligence. Here's an odd coincidence. I'm a part-owner of the building where he has his offices."

"You've met him before."

"No. First time I saw him was the funeral."

She didn't believe in coincidence. It seemed far more likely that Vargas knew about his relationship to Latimer and solidified the connection by being his landlord. "Do you own many buildings like his?"

"I'm part of an investment group that owns forty-seven commercial properties in and around Denver," he said. "Which leads me to a proposition I wanted to discuss with you."

"Proposition?"

In her ear, Blake said, "Don't let him get you off track. Bring him back to the study."

There might have been a clever way to navigate these waters and lead the conversation back to the study, but she lacked that skill, especially when facing somebody like Vargas. With his business talent, he must have been a genius when it came to negotiations.

Her only ploy was being direct. "No proposition. Not now. I want to talk more about the study."

His smile was pure charm. "Whatever you want. Ask your questions."

"About Prentice's data," she said. "I'd like to take a look at the DNA profiles."

"Give me your e-mail, and I'll send a copy as soon as I get back to my office."

It occurred to her that he'd hacked into Prentice's files and was likely to do the same to hers. Not that she had any deep, dark secrets in her personal files. But the loss of privacy concerned her.

Still, she wrote down her e-mail address and passed it across the white linen tablecloth toward him. When he took it, their fingers touched and a spark raced up her arm. This wasn't sexual energy like she had with Blake. Vargas felt dangerous, as though their shared DNA gave him too much access to her inner thoughts. Of course, that was untrue. He couldn't know what she was thinking or feeling, unless…unless he'd also taken a look at the psychological information obtained by Blake's father during their annual interview. He must have done so; he wouldn't leave that stone unturned.

She asked, "What did you find when you hacked into Dr. Ray's records?"

"Very little." He didn't bother denying her implied accusation. "Blake's father wasn't a high-tech person. He didn't keep information on his computer."

But he'd used a laptop which had been stolen from

his office, indicating that the killer thought it had value. "Maybe you didn't look in the right files."

"Not a chance. I'm thorough," he said. "Think about it, Eve. When you did interviews with him, he made notes on a yellow legal pad. Right?"

"That's true. And the annual surveys we filled out were always in printed form."

She leaned back in her chair as their meal arrived. Her chicken salad was excellent.

In her ear, Blake said, "I hear you crunching. You're eating, aren't you? Damn, I'm hungry."

She made yummy sounds to tease him. "Mmm. This is the best chicken I've ever had."

Blake moaned. "You're killing me."

"Perfectly seasoned." She smacked her lips. "Tasty."

With a puzzled expression, Vargas studied her. "It's nice to see a woman who enjoys her food."

"I bet you date a lot of skinny supermodel types who don't eat at all."

"Good bet," he said.

In her ear, Blake muttered, "Get back to the topic."

Purely to annoy him, she said, "I could eat all day. I could order some dessert, maybe cheesecake or chocolate brownies or everything on the menu."

"Whatever you want," Vargas said.

Looking across the table at him, she gestured with her fork. "You said there wasn't much on Dr. Ray's computer. Tell me what you found."

"A statistical abstract with all the areas of study encoded. Without the key, all I could discern was that Dr. Ray discovered some correlations between DNA and certain behaviors."

"Like what?"

"Psychological traits, like introversion or extroversion. Or skill sets, such as our shared proclivity for numbers."

"Or talents," she said, thinking of the musical abilities displayed by Vargas, Latimer and Pyro. "But these traits weren't labeled?"

"If you like, I can send you the abstract."

"Great." Once she had these numerical samplings, she might be able to learn more about the study results. She was good at cracking codes. "I'd like to see Dr. Ray's personal analysis. To see what my behaviors said about me."

"I'm surprised that you trust psychology. Genetics is more scientific."

"True enough, but I believe that we make our own decisions. Genetics might have given me an ability in math, but I chose to study it."

"Our lives start with DNA. It's the most important factor in determining our course."

"I can't blame genetics for my personal choices, which happened to include watching every single episode of *Star Trek: The Next Generation*. I had a huge crush on Commander Data."

"The android who longed to have human feelings," he said. "An interesting choice."

"I wanted to help him. To be the woman who made him smile and laugh and fall in love."

"You're a romantic," he said. "Looking for a soul mate."

Before she met Blake, she would have scoffed at the idea of soul mates. Now, she wasn't so sure. The way she responded to him didn't make logical sense. "With all the possible mating combinations, it's statistically unlikely that one particular man and one particular woman are destined to be together."

"What about you and Blake?" he asked.

Am I that obvious? "What about us?"

"Genetically, it seems likely that you'd be well-matched."

His questions and perceptions were throwing her way off balance. In her ear, Blake warned, "Don't respond. Keep the focus on him. And the study."

"Enough about me," she said. "What about your secrets? What did you tell Dr. Ray?"

"I always felt different," he said. "Which was fine with me. I expect others to come up to my standards."

"If they don't?"

He didn't answer her question. Instead, he sipped his wine and changed the subject. "Now that I've found you, Eve, I want to spend more time together. I want to know you."

"And if I don't measure up to your standards?"

"You will," he said.

If she'd set out to choose a half brother, she would have looked for someone more empathetic and forthcoming. Vargas drew her toward him with his natural magnetism, but he was the opposite of warm and cuddly. If she wasn't worthy of his standards, she had no doubt that he'd throw her under the bus.

"How's your relationship with your parents?" she asked. "By parents, I mean the people who raised you."

"Positive. As you know, I've been financially successful. I've taken care of Mom and Dad, bought them a house in Florida."

"What about your genetic parents," she asked, returning to another topic he'd skillfully sidestepped. "Have you made a search for them?"

"How could I? All I have is their DNA."

She didn't believe him. Vargas believed that genetics

determined behavior and achievement. He would have desperately wanted to find his biological parents, would have spared no expense in hiring experts and hackers. "Did you look into the DNA databases?" she asked. "The military has pretty extensive records. Or CODIS."

"I hired a researcher. He didn't find anything." Dismissively, he brushed away that topic. "Are you ready to hear my proposal?"

"Sure."

"Like you, I support ecological causes, and I appreciate the work you're doing at Sun Wave on alternative energy sources." When he grinned, she noticed that he had a dimple in his right cheek. Just as she did. "Being green might be a family trait."

"Most intelligent people realize the importance of saving the planet."

"True," he said. "I'd like to offer several of my properties to be used as Sun Wave alternate energy prototypes. And I'll cover the cost for the installations."

"That's very generous."

"And not a bad tax write-off." He raised his glass to her. "Here's to working together."

Though she felt as though he was manipulating her, she couldn't refuse. At Sun Wave, they'd run into obstacles when it came to setting up prototypes for solar energy. She raised her water glass and clinked her rim with his. "I can't say no."

"We're partners," he said. "Brother and sister."

He seemed to be claiming her as a possession. Her shoulders tensed. Vargas might be involved in Dr. Ray's murder. He might even have pulled the trigger himself. She had to get out of there before she blurted an accusation. "Much as I'd like dessert, I have somewhere else I need to be. As I'm sure you do."

When she rose to say goodbye, he hugged her. "We're family, Eve. If there's anything you want, anything at all, call me."

Outside, the bright afternoon sun warmed her face and thawed her tension. She felt like a fly that had escaped the spider's web. Vargas might be her half brother, but he wasn't necessarily her friend.

She looked down the two-lane street with cars parked on both sides. An hour ago, she'd left Blake outside a specialty tea shop. He was nowhere in sight. "Blake? Where are you?"

In her ear, he responded. "Turn left and keep walking. Don't worry. I'm nearby."

"Where?"

"Play along with him," Blake instructed.

"Who?"

"Just do it."

Why was he so cryptic? Just once, she'd appreciate an explanation from him instead of a terse command. *Just do it?* She pivoted, went to her left as he'd ordered and walked. There wasn't much of a crowd on the sidewalk—a couple of business types, shoppers who were visiting the boutiques, tourists—nobody who appeared to be dangerous.

She'd only gone a couple of steps when Latimer's driver, Randall, stepped out of a doorway and blocked her path.

Chapter Thirteen

Blake had been aware of Randall's presence for the past half hour. He'd been watching from the opposite side of the street when the stocky, balding man had come around the corner, stopped at the entrance to the Gilpin Grill and peeked inside. After speaking on a cell phone, Randall had gone to a stone bench beside a planter filled with orange and yellow geraniums where he'd sat, waiting and making no attempt to hide.

Blake had concluded that Randall was the messenger. But what the hell was the message? Obviously, Latimer's driver had come to the Gilpin Grill to see Eve. How did he know where to find her? Had Vargas tipped him off to the location? The idea of Vargas and Latimer working together worried him.

Instead of a direct confrontation, Blake had decided to hold off and see what unfolded. As he had listened to Eve's conversation with Vargas through his earpiece, he had stayed out of Randall's sightlines. His military experience had schooled him in methods to make himself invisible. Less than a month ago, he'd led a covert rescue operation in a Pakistani city. Dodging through those narrow streets had been easier than blending into this upscale warren of shops and restaurants.

He had maneuvered into a position where he could study

Latimer's chauffeur. Randall was heavy but not flabby. His broad shoulders and upper arms stretched the seams on his lightweight sports jacket. When he had turned his face upward to catch the sun, Blake had noticed his misshapen nose, a couple of scars and a cauliflower ear. At one time in his life, Randall might have been a boxer, and he would have been the kind of fighter who put his head down and came at you like a tank—unstoppable, capable of taking punishment and of dishing it out.

When Eve had come out of the restaurant and followed his directions, she was face-to face-with Randall. She smiled and said, "This is a coincidence."

Blake was close enough that the sound of her normal voice harmonized with the tinny echo from his earpiece.

"Good afternoon," Randall said. "Will you come with me, please? Dr. Latimer is waiting."

They crossed the street at the four-way stop sign and walked north. They made an odd couple. Beauty and the beast, Blake thought as he watched the sway of her hips. Eve seemed to get prettier every time he saw her; she was definitely growing on him. His desires were complicated by her admission that she was a virgin. If they made love, he'd be damn sure that was what she wanted.

Within a block, the shops had faded into an expensive residential area with massive private homes and classy town houses. Through the earpiece, Blake warned her, "Whatever you do, don't get in the car."

Still on the opposite side of the street, he narrowed the physical distance between them.

Through Eve's listening device, he heard Randall ask, "Do you know where Blake is?"

"I can honestly say that I don't." Eve sounded annoyed. "Do you mind telling me what we're doing?"

"Dr. Latimer would have come by himself, but he's having a bad day."

Blake wasn't surprised. After they had left his house last night, Latimer had seemed panicky. The stress couldn't be good for his illness.

Randall approached the heavy bronze Cadillac that they'd seen him driving last night and opened the door.

From this angle, Blake couldn't see the interior of the car. He watched as Eve braced her arm against the roof and peered inside. "Hello, Dr. Latimer. What's this about?"

Latimer responded, "Please get in."

She stood up straight. "It's such a lovely day. Why don't you step out here and we can talk."

"I need to conserve my strength."

Blake saw Randall move into position. One shove from him and Eve would be in the car. He had to prevent that action. Stepping into the open, he shouted, "There you are."

He jogged across the street.

Quietly, Randall stepped back. For a husky man, he was talented at fading into his surroundings. Blake reminded himself that silent threats were often the most deadly.

He approached Eve and gave her a little hug, subtly removing her earpiece. "I thought you were going to wait for me outside the Grill."

"Well, I ran into Randall."

Blake leaned down and greeted Latimer. "Nice to see you."

"Please," he said, "get in the car. Both of you."

Latimer looked like hell. Behind his thick glasses, his eyes were sunken. Greasy strands of blond hair plastered across his forehead.

Blake nodded to Eve. "You sit back here. I'll stay up front with Randall."

If the driver tried anything, Blake would be ready for him. Once situated in the passenger seat, he turned and looked into the back.

Though the weather was pleasantly warm, Latimer shuddered inside a shawl-like sweater. His lips barely parted as he spoke. "Finding out about my biological parents was difficult for me. Devastating." He drew a ragged breath. "My father—the man who raised me—provided me with a very good life. When I chose medicine instead of the family business, he encouraged my dream, sent me to the best schools, arranged for mentors. He's a good man. The best."

"I understand," Blake said. "Ray Jantzen is the only father I've ever known, the only man I want to be my father."

"My work with infertility involves genetics," Latimer said. "In a way, that makes it harder for me to accept that the man who raised me isn't my father."

"Sure he is," Eve said. "Real parenting involves nurturing. Laughter and squabbles. Pain and happiness. That's what makes a parent. Love is more important than biology."

He couldn't believe the supremely practical Eve would be touting the value of relationships and love. This was a woman who relied on facts, not emotions. If his dad had been able to hear her talking about relationships and nurturing, he would have been proud.

"I know," Latimer said, "that you're trying to locate the list of genetic parents."

"The information is pertinent to my dad's murder," Blake said.

Latimer stared at him. "My father must never know that we're not of the same blood."

"I don't see a problem," Eve said. "There's no reason why he should be informed."

Blake knew the decision wasn't theirs to make. By not informing the parents, Prentice had committed fraud. A crime. A prosecutable offense. There was an obligation to bring the truth to light. "If the police are involved, we can't control the outcome."

"I've already spoken to Pyro," Latimer said. "Though he appears to be delighted that his father isn't really his father, he promised me that my family wouldn't be brought into it. Can you do the same? Continue your search, but erase my name from the list."

Which would be committing yet another fraud. "I can't make that promise."

"What if I made it worth your while?" Latimer shifted in the backseat. The slight movement caused him to wince as though his bones were sore. "I can arrange for you to meet with Prentice."

A tempting offer. But as soon as Latimer spoke, Blake knew he was dealing with a liar. Last night, Latimer had claimed that he didn't know the whereabouts of Prentice. Dealing with all these superbabies was like playing chess with several genius partners. Latimer had his agenda. Vargas had another plan. Every move had a countermove until the final checkmate. "How well do you know David Vargas?"

"I don't."

Blake looked toward Randall. "If Vargas didn't tell you, how did you know that Eve would be at the Gilpin Grill?"

Randall stared through the windshield. His meaty hands rested on the steering wheel as though he was driving. "I dropped a GPS tracking device in her purse."

"What?" Eve erupted from the backseat. "Why do people keep bugging me?"

With a shrug, Randall said, "I thought it might be useful to know your movements."

"We weren't spying on you," Latimer assured her. "We didn't even turn it on until after I'd talked to Prentice this morning."

Her blue eyes narrowed in an angry glare. For a woman who claimed to be logical, she had a lot of passion seething under the surface. She snarled, "I must have called Prentice a dozen times and he won't pick up. Why did he take your call?"

"I don't know," Latimer said.

"I don't believe it. And I don't believe that you aren't in touch with Vargas. He's part-owner of the building where you have your offices."

Latimer seemed to retreat deeper into his illness. "My office lease is handled by a Realtor. I've never met this person you're talking about."

Eve seemed to assess his response and find it rational. She still wasn't letting Latimer off the hook. "Where's Prentice? Where is he taking this supposed vacation?"

"He's not vacationing," Latimer said. "He's in hiding."

"From what?"

"Isn't it obvious?" Latimer said. "He's been threatened."

"Who's after him?"

"He didn't give me a name." With an effort, Latimer straightened his shoulders. "Will you work with me? Do everything you can to delete my name from the list?"

"I'll try," Blake said. "Tell me more about Prentice."

"He didn't go into great detail, but he told me that he'd performed an IVF procedure for a great deal of money.

Though he successfully implanted the embryo, the father turned on him."

It didn't take much to read between the lines. Prentice was talking about Eve's pregnancy. "Who's the father?"

"I don't have a name." Latimer turned to Eve. "I assume you're the mother. Do you know the father of your baby?"

She waved her hands in front of her face, erasing his question. "Prentice did this to me for money?"

"A great deal of money," Latimer said. "His clinic in Aspen has an extremely high overhead. These are difficult financial times for everyone."

Eve's anger went out of her. She slouched back against the car seat. "Why?"

"You can ask Prentice yourself," Latimer said. "Tomorrow night at my office. Eight o'clock. That's all I can tell you. Now, I need to go home."

So did Blake. He needed time to think. Prentice wasn't involved in a scheme to develop a race of superbabies. He'd implanted Eve for a cash settlement. Money. The oldest motive in the book.

LEAVING LATIMER BEHIND, Eve shuffled along the sidewalk beside Blake. She was frustrated and mad as hell. She couldn't believe how much had been thrown at her. Everything—lock, stock and...baby.

Because of factors beyond her control, she was a pregnant virgin. An unwilling pregnant virgin. An unwilling pregnant virgin who was attracted to a man who might be her brother. Worst of all, the unknown father of her baby was a crazy person, possibly homicidal.

The only way her life could get worse was if armed thugs were after her. Oh, wait! They were.

She grumbled, "I want a weapon."

"I thought you wanted to learn hand-to-hand combat."

"I do. And I also want a gun."

"Feeling like shooting somebody?"

"Several somebodies," she said, "starting with Prentice. Can you believe he messed up my life for a paycheck?"

"A really big paycheck," Blake said.

"I don't care if it was a million dollars. He had no right to violate me. This sounds crazy, but I would have felt better if my pregnancy was part of an experiment. You know, creating the next generation of superbabies."

"Maybe it is. We don't know the motives for your baby daddy."

They approached the supersleek Mercedes, and he gallantly opened the door for her.

She eyed him suspiciously. "Why so gentlemanly?"

"After your fancy lunch with Vargas, I figured I better step up my game."

"Vargas? Sure, he's got money and class and isn't bad to look at, but you're…" Teasing, she patted Blake's clean-shaven cheek. "You're you."

"What's that mean?"

"Don't go fishing for compliments, Mr. Perfect."

While she nestled into the soft leather seats, he went around to the trunk where he kept his arsenal. When he got into the car, he handed her a plastic device that was about the size of a remote control with two pincers on the end.

"Stun gun," he said. "Flip this switch to activate, press the business end against your attacker and pull the trigger. Nobody gets killed, but it stops an assailant in their tracks."

"I like it." She squeezed the plastic handle. "Like *Star Trek* when you set your phaser to stun."

"Don't set it off by accident. That's several hundred thousand volts, and it really hurts."

When she went to stash her weapon in her purse, she remembered that Randall had dropped a GPS tracker in her shoulder bag. As Blake eased away from the curb, she dumped the contents onto the floor in front of her. Hunched over, she shifted through her wallet, sunglasses, various receipts, an emery board, cell phone, lipstick and various other detritus until she found the small round disc. "Aha!"

"Do I want to know what you're doing?"

"Making sure Latimer doesn't know where we are." She lowered the window and tossed it into the street, hoping that it would be picked up by a squirrel and hidden away forever. "Okay, where do we go from here?"

"I was hoping for an excuse to drive this fine vehicle to Aspen, but Prentice is coming to us. No need to track him down."

"Unless Latimer pulls a double cross." She didn't think he'd take that chance. Hiding his genetic secret from his parents seemed important to him. "He really looked miserable."

"Don't let sympathy cloud your thinking," Blake warned.

"I won't." She pushed aside her emotional reaction. "Just the facts. Latimer has a tenuous connection to Vargas through the lease on his building. And he knows Pyro. And he lied to us about not being able to reach Prentice. However, he seemed truly shocked when we told him about his genetic parents."

"Or was he shocked that we knew?"

"A possibility," she conceded.

"We can't trust him. When we go to his office, we'll be prepared for an ambush."

He stopped short to avoid a careless driver, then reached out and patted the dashboard. He murmured, "That's okay, Ms. Mercedes. I won't let anything happen to you."

He wasn't trying to charm her, not like Vargas, but Blake drew her like a magnet. She wanted to ruffle his hair or give him a little kiss on the cheek. "You still haven't told me our plan for this afternoon."

"First, I want to go back to the house and find the box of stuff from the clinic at Fitzsimons. It sounded like Dr. Puller and Connie cleared off his desk pretty quickly. There might be a clue."

"We have lots of other research to do. Vargas promised to send me the results of his hacking into Prentice's and your dad's computer."

Blake reminded her, "He also said there were no names attached."

"I'm good at breaking codes."

She flipped open her cell phone to check her e-mail messages. Nothing from Vargas. But there was a message from General Walsh. It had to be Blake's DNA results.

Her fingers trembled above the keys. Finally, she'd have her answer. She'd know if she and Blake were brother and sister.

Chapter Fourteen

At the house, Eve set up her computer at the desk in Blake's bedroom where she could use his printer. After these anxious hours of wondering, she was almost afraid to compare their DNA profiles.

Before Blake barged into her life, she hadn't felt like she was missing anything by not having a relationship. Her work was enough. She was happy as a single person. Not lonely, not really. But now she was different. Irrational, crazy emotions intruded into her life equation. She wanted to be with him, and she knew he felt the same way about her. If it turned out that they were genetically related, they had a problem.

With a few clicks on the keyboard, she opened the e-mail from General Walsh's secretary. When the DNA chart appeared, she sat and stared blankly.

Blake hovered at her shoulder. "What are you waiting for?"

"Does it really matter what it says? It's only genetics. Even if it turns out wrong…"

"Damn it, Eve. Read the charts."

She printed out his DNA results to compare with her own. "These profiles aren't detailed or conclusive. They couldn't be used in court to determine paternity."

"But they're close enough to tell if we're related. Right?"

"I'm not a genetics expert. I'm remembering information that my friend, Hugo the MonkeyMan, explained to me when I helped him coordinate his study." Sometimes her eidetic memory came in handy. "These charts will show thirteen core STR loci and their chromosomal positions as well as twenty-five alleles."

"In English," he said.

"It's like a fingerprint. With the exception of identical twins, nobody has the same DNA. However, family relationships can be determined through comparison of the—"

"Just do it."

She placed the two sheets of paper side by side. There were zero matches and few similarities. Yes! There was no genetic reason to keep them apart. "I'm not your sister. Not your half sister. We're not related."

He pulled her out of the chair and into his arms. "Then it's okay if I do this."

His mouth pressed hard against hers. At first, she was surprised by the intensity of his kiss. She'd never been ravaged before but suspected that this was what it felt like. Exciting. Confusing.

Her heartbeat accelerated, and her blood rushed. She could almost hear the surging as a fierce energy swept through her. She clung to him, pressing herself so tightly against his chest that she felt as if they were merging into one being.

They toppled backward onto his queen-size bed, and the air left her lungs. She was breathless, literally gasping.

He rose above her, and she looked up into his coffee brown eyes, perfectly spaced. His lips parted, not smiling but inviting her.

She flung her arms around his neck and dragged him down on top of her, welcoming the crush of his full weight.

He rolled to his side, still holding her. "Gently," he said. "I want this to last."

Why should they go slow? Her heart was racing, and her decision was made. Blake was the man who would take her virginity. "Am I doing something wrong?"

He traced the line of her jaw. "Usually, it's the guy who wants to go fast."

"Like I told you, I'm not exactly what you'd call experienced."

"Virgin territory." He smiled. "Are you sure you're ready?"

"Why not? I'm already pregnant."

His eyes darkened. "What Prentice did to you is unthinkable. I'm sorry you have to go through this."

It didn't seem as bad when she was with him. "The worst part is that I have no frame of reference. I don't know how to be pregnant. There must be vitamins I should take. Should I go to a doctor to make sure everything is all right?"

"Whatever you need, I'll support you."

She believed him. "Thanks."

"The last thing I want is to hurt you. Are you sure about making love?"

He cradled her in his arms, comforting her with surprising gentleness and kindness. Blake was a man's man, an alpha male who naturally took charge. This empathy showed another side of him. Not only did he care about her, but he actually seemed to understand how she felt.

A tear spilled down her cheek. There hadn't been time for her to cry, and she didn't want to start weeping now.

She wiped it away. "I want to make love. I want to know what it's like."

As he stroked her shoulders and tenderly rocked her in his arms, she let go of the anger and emotional pain she'd been holding in check. Prentice had stolen a precious part of her life—the natural progression of courtship and love that resulted in creating a baby. A heavy sob tore from her gut, and her tears flowed. More emotion than she'd felt in her entire life broke free in a torrent.

Blake absorbed her outburst. He murmured while she sobbed and cursed. He held her and waited until the storm abated to a whimper and she subsided into a quiet aftermath.

She sighed. "I didn't know that was in me."

"It's okay."

When he smiled at her, she turned her face away. "I must be a mess."

"You look good to me."

Yeah, sure. She knew her eyes were red. Her face, blotchy. "I'd like to wash up."

He rose from the bed and pulled her to her feet. Then he took her arm as though he was escorting her to a grand ball instead of to the bathroom down the hall. As she walked beside him, her step was light, buoyant. Her tears had washed away the anxiety that weighed upon her.

In the bathroom, he lifted her and sat her on the countertop beside the sink. She should have told him that she was facing the wrong way and needed the mirror to clean up, but she was curious about what he intended to do.

He turned on the faucet and dampened a washcloth. "Close your eyes, Eve."

The warm cloth stroked her forehead and cheeks. He lightly kissed her lips, washed again and patted her face dry.

She felt his hands glide down her black denim pants to her feet. When he removed her shoes and socks, her toes curled. "What are you doing?"

"I always feel clean after my feet are washed."

When he stroked her instep, a shiver raced up her legs. She opened her eyes and looked down at him, kneeling before her like the prince with Cinderella. This wasn't how she thought making love would be, but she liked it.

The warm washcloth caressed her toes. She closed her eyes again and leaned back, enjoying the sensations that raced through her. Though he touched only her feet, a tingling started in the pit of her stomach. She was aroused, very definitely aroused.

"You have pretty feet," he said as he dried her feet. "Pink, little toes."

She truly wished that she'd had a pedicure. "You've seen my feet before. When I was wearing my sandals."

"Now they're naked."

Which was exactly what she wanted to be. Completely naked. When he stood, she looked him straight in the face. "I should take off my T-shirt so you can wash my chest."

He pulled the T-shirt over her head. His eyes warmed as he gazed down at her. She loved the way he was looking at her, with relish and approval.

His thumb touched the pi tattoo above her left breast. "I like it."

"On second thought," she said, "I should wash you, too."

With quick dexterity, she unbuttoned his shirt and pushed it off his shoulder. His T-shirt came next. His muscular chest with a light sprinkle of hair was, of course, perfect. On his flexed bicep the tattoo of Icarus looked like fine art.

"Another thought." Her voice had taken on a husky tone. "Forget the washcloth and kiss me."

He parted her thighs and stepped between them. It felt natural to wrap her legs around him and to embrace him as they kissed. His flesh was warm, and the friction of their bodies generated even more heat. In a matter of minutes, she'd gone from weeping to an amazing excitement with too many sensations to count.

Her primal brain—the hypothalamus—took over, and instinct ruled her behavior. Every touch, every sense and taste had a distinct clarity. Though unaware of why she was doing what she was doing, she knew that he liked to be touched in the crook of his elbow and kissed on his earlobe.

He unfastened her bra to fondle her breasts. When he flicked her nipple with his thumb, a hum of pleasure purred through her. Contented but greedy, she wanted more.

With her legs still wrapped around him, he lifted her off the countertop and carried her down the hall to the bedroom, where they stretched out on the bed.

Though she wanted to take mental snapshots of every second, she couldn't concentrate when he rained kisses over her eager body. Before she realized what was happening, their clothes were gone and they were under the sheets.

Boldly, she grasped his hot erection. When she tugged, he shuddered.

"Slow down, Eve."

"Why do you keep saying that?"

"Because I want this to be good for you. I want you to be ready for me."

She really didn't know how she could be more ready. Sensations zinged through her, and she could feel them building to a crescendo. Still, she lay back on the sheets.

"I guess I should ask about condoms. I'm already pregnant, but—"

"I've been tested recently. I'm clean. You?"

"Um, virgin."

"Right. No condom required."

As he held her gaze, his hand slipped down her body to the juncture of her thighs. When he parted the sensitive folds, she gasped. *Oh, my God, this is really happening.* His finger entered her, and she thought she was going to burst.

"Slowly," he whispered.

The only way she could keep from exploding was by reciting prime numbers in her head. She only got to twenty-three. "Now, Blake. I want you inside me. Now."

He poised above her. Then, with a thrust, he filled her. She arched to meet him, and their passion took on a fierce rhythm, driving toward an ecstasy she'd never felt before. A final thrust and then all the clichés were true. The fireworks. The perfect harmony. The incredible release.

Blake shuddered above her. He fell onto the sheets beside her. When she looked at him, he was beaming.

A residual tremor rippled through her and she reveled in the sensations.

When her breathing returned to something like normal, Blake was watching her. His dark, sexy eyes glittered as he asked, "How was it?"

She stroked his tat. "I have no basis for comparison."

"How did you feel?"

"Like every cell in my body was about to explode, and then I had what I'd identify as an orgasm. Maybe more than one. Is that right?"

"That's correct." He ran his thumb across her lips. "You must be happy. You're smiling."

"Must be." She couldn't help teasing him. "It could have been better. Everything improves with practice."

"Don't worry, Eve. We'll be doing this again." He kissed her. "And again."

She snuggled into his arms. Beyond his shoulder, she saw daylight streaking through the drawn blinds in his bedroom. "It's not even five o'clock. We still have things to do today."

"No rush."

They were meeting Prentice tomorrow night at Latimer's office, and she wanted to be prepared. "We came here to look for the box of your father's things that Connie brought over from Fitzsimons."

"You're right."

He kissed her forehead and rose from the bed. For a moment, she lay back and simply stared at his well-proportioned body. The ratio of his shoulders to his lean hips amazed her. Even though she wasn't an artist, she appreciated the strength and sheer beauty of the male form. She would never forget this moment, this perfect moment.

"Your dad was right," she said.

"About what?"

"He kept encouraging me to open up and have relationships. He said I'd enjoy them." She remembered Dr. Ray's kind smile as he listened to her compare herself to a prime number that didn't need anyone else. "Do you think if we'd met earlier, you and I would have been attracted?"

"I don't look back and think of what might have been." He pulled on his cargo pants. "Always move forward."

"Spoken like a trooper," she said.

Though she agreed that the present was the only firm basis for understanding, she couldn't help speculating. What would happen to her precious new relationship with

Blake when they found his father's murderer? A quick analysis of probability told her that they would part and go their separate ways. She doubted that he'd quit the Special Forces to stay with her, especially since she was pregnant.

When she was dressed, she followed him into the attached double garage where the Mercedes filled the space left by his dad's station wagon. Blake caressed the roof as he circled around the car. "I don't have high hopes for finding useful evidence in this stuff. Dad only spent one afternoon a week at Fitzsimons."

"But he knew that people were after information about the study. He might have chosen the most unlikely place to hide it."

"I think I put the box back here, under the workbench."

"Did your dad do building projects?"

"He tried. But he wasn't much good as a handyman."

She remembered that Vargas had pointed out Dr. Ray's reluctance to use new technology. "And he didn't particularly like computers."

"He was an old-fashioned guy."

Blake lifted a box onto the workbench and started taking things out: a cactus, a wide assortment of pens, a calculator with extra-large numerals and a misshapen ceramic bowl.

Eve picked up the vase. "Did you make this?"

"A second-grade project. Art isn't one of my talents. Nor is music. Nor making money like Vargas." He turned toward her. "Are we sure that my genetic parents were outstanding individuals?"

She nodded. "Your gifts are physical. You excelled in sports. You're in the Special Forces. And you can throw a knife with pinpoint accuracy."

"Ha! I knew you were impressed when I did that."

She glided her hand down his back and patted his butt. "Not to mention your skill in making love."

"That's genetic?"

"You inherited your physical attributes and your stamina," she said. "But there's an emotional component. I'm not sure what Dr. Ray would call it."

"Empathy." From the box, he took out a framed photograph that was a duplicate of the one in his office. "Me and Mom. Dad loved this picture. I never knew why he didn't update it. He always said this photo was the key to his happiness."

An interesting phrase. "The key?"

Blake glanced up sharply. "He said it several times."

"Take it out of the frame."

Blake unfastened the backing on the frame. Written on the flip side of the photograph were twenty-four names and twenty-four corresponding numbers.

Chapter Fifteen

Blake turned the photograph over in his hands, impressed by his dad's cleverness and irritated at himself for not figuring out the clue sooner. "He gave me the answer. The key."

Eve nodded. "Dr. Ray must have known for a long time that the information generated by the study was dangerous."

"He should have told me." Though Blake didn't claim genius status when it came to intellectual stuff, he was damned good in a fight. "Why the hell didn't he call on me for help?"

"Because this was his battle."

She was blunt but accurate. Blake nodded. "He thought he could handle it by himself."

"Also, he didn't want to tell you about your genetic parents."

"Why? It wouldn't have changed the way I felt about him."

Her clear blue eyes softened. "I'm the wrong person to ask when it comes to motives, but I'd guess that your dad's rationale for keeping this secret had something to do with his love for you."

He wished he could go back in time to when his father was alive and tell him how much he loved him and respected him. Ray Jantzen was the best father any man could have.

He handed the photo to her. "Now what?"

"We check my computer to see if Vargas fulfilled his promise and sent the DNA charts and your dad's statistical abstracts."

He followed her into the house. The twenty-four names they had just discovered were a list of suspects—people who would kill to keep the information contained in the Prentice-Jantzen study a secret. But Blake had the feeling they'd already encountered the man who murdered his father. Trevor Latimer. David Vargas. Or Pyro.

In his bedroom, Eve pounced on the laptop computer. Her slender fingers skipped across the keyboard as she pulled up e-mails. "Oh, good. Here's the stuff from Vargas."

While she opened the file and studied what looked like an incomprehensible array of data, he sprawled on the bed. The linens were disheveled from their lovemaking, and it seemed like a waste of time to straighten the sheets. He fully intended to mess them up again.

With Eve, once was definitely not enough. She sure as hell didn't make love with the shyness of a virgin. She was demanding in a good way, curious and sexy and passionate.

She hunched over the computer. Deciphering the data was her bailiwick. There was nothing he could do right now, except wait.

"Vargas sent the charts." She spun around in the swivel chair. "Dr. Ray's key gives us names for the subjects. That's the good news."

"And the bad?"

"Number one—there are no names for the genetic parents. Number two—your father's data can't be interpreted without knowing what he was testing for."

"Behavior." Seemed obvious to Blake. "Dad used his annual questionnaire to assess behavior."

"All those questions." She rolled her eyes. "Do you prefer a party or a quiet evening alone? Do you work better on your own or when being given clear direction? How many times do you have sex in a week?"

"I never answered that one," he said.

"Awkward for you." She started the printer. "I really hated the 'on a scale of one to ten' section. Are you a happy person? A self-starter? Fearful?"

When he was a child, filling out the annual questionnaire had been a game. The older he got, the more he had resented the questions. Still, the results interested him. "Are you sure you can't read the data?"

"It's a statistical analysis on a graph. All numbers."

"Which you love."

"I do, indeed." Her smile was cute and sexy at the same time. "Unfortunately, words are sometimes necessary. It appears that your father rated thirty-two behaviors for each subject. But he didn't label the behaviors."

"Come again?"

"We need another key."

Each layer of complication piled on top of the one before. If Eve hadn't been helping him, he'd have gone berserk by now. "I guess that means I need to search. What am I looking for?"

"A list of behavioral characteristics. You know, like introversion and extroversion. Or depression. Stuff like that. There are thirty-two."

He rolled off the bed and stretched his arms over his head. Impatience built inside him. He longed for action. "I'll start in Dad's office."

First, he went to the kitchen and opened the fridge. All he'd had to eat since breakfast was gelato, but the array of plastic containers filled with funeral casseroles was downright depressing. He threw together a sandwich from cold cuts and devoured it as he walked down the hallway.

In the doorway, he stopped. Entering the room where his father had been killed shouldn't have bothered him. He'd been in and out of here dozens of times. This moment was different because he'd been thinking about Dad, feeling the ache of losing him.

His sandwich tasted like dust in his mouth. He tossed half of it into the trash can. His dad and mom had loved this house, and he had good memories of family time together. A sense of bittersweet nostalgia enveloped him.

He needed to make this right. No matter how impossible it seemed, he would find the killer. When he did, he'd gut this room and start over. Nope, that wasn't enough. The hell with redecorating; he'd sell the house. With both parents gone, there was no reason to stay in Denver. Except for Eve. He wanted to spend more time with her, and it didn't seem right to abandon her while she was pregnant.

Thinking of her grounded him. She'd given him a job to do: find the key.

He pawed the stuff on his dad's desk. The obvious hiding place was the photograph of him and his mom—an exact duplicate of the one he'd had at his office.

Blake detached the backing and found nothing but a photo. He ran his finger around the edge of the frame, feeling for an encoded chip or microdot. As if his dad, who could barely handle e-mail, would use such a sophisticated device.

To find the answer, he had to think of Ray Jantzen, the man who had raised him. Blake whispered, "Where is it, Dad?"

He could almost hear a reply. *Think, Blake. Don't rush. Take your time.*

Though the desk was cluttered, his dad's thinking followed methodical patterns that made it harder than hell to put anything over on him. Blake clearly recalled one of his father's interrogations after he'd stayed out past curfew. The questions went from how he'd lost track of time to how much he'd been drinking. Their final discussion always seemed to circle back to Blake's tendency to take risks. *Look before you leap.* How many times had his dad said that? "Excessive Risk-Taking" was probably one of the personality behaviors on his chart.

He started opening file folders and thumbing through the contents. His dad's words jumped out at him. An intellectual tone, sometimes stuffy, was apparent in the typed pages of articles he prepared for publication and speeches for presentation at conferences. More revealing were the doodles and scribbled notes in the margins that ranged from "boring" to a row of exclamation points.

In one paper, "Correlation of High Intelligence and Anti-Social Personality Disorder," his father had jotted the initials *P.G.* in the margin. Peter Gregory? The coauthor was listed as Ryan Puller.

Might be useful to give that shrink a call.

AS EVE PORED OVER THE genetic charts, relationships became clear. Her own DNA profile showed that she didn't have any matches for both mother and father, but she shared a mother with Vargas, the other female and two other people whose names she didn't recognize from the Condolence Book. Blake's genetic mother also provided eggs for four other subjects.

To clarify the interrelationships of the genetic fathers, she laid out graphs and variation equations. Vargas appeared to be the only subject who had a singular genetic father.

Then she turned to Dr. Ray's charts of behaviors rated between one and ten. In her psychological profile, most rankings ranged between three and five, which appeared to be in the normal range. One spiked to an eight. Because she was an introvert? Or had ability in math?

Two names had an unusual number of eights and nines, probably indicating extreme behavior. One was Vargas, who probably considered the high numbers to be a mark of achievement. The other was Pyro. Despite their similar behavior patterns, they didn't share genetic traits. Interesting. These statistics might be proof of Dr. Ray's theory that upbringing was more important in personality development than DNA. As she'd told Vargas, it was all about choices.

Blake's profile had an eight and a couple of sixes. She traced her finger down the list of his characteristics. For the first time in her life, she wished for words instead of numbers. She wanted to know what he was thinking *and feeling.* He'd made love to her with such incredible gentleness. How much did he really care about her? As much as she cared about him?

She frowned at the charts in her hand as she swiveled back and forth in the desk chair. Spending time with Blake had been fun. Making love had been amazing. But relationships had a downside. There would come a moment when they said goodbye. And she'd miss him.

"Ha!" He charged into the room. Energy sparked around him like lightning bolts. Whatever he'd found in his father's office must have been significant.

"I really hope," she said, "that you've got solid information for me."

"I just got off the phone with Dr. Puller. He and my

dad collaborated on a thesis about high intelligence and antisocial personality disorder. Bottom line—smart people make good sociopaths."

"Define sociopath."

"Criminal mastermind."

"Now you're getting into my territory." She grinned. "Criminal masterminds are necessary for epic fantasy battles between the forces of good and evil. But I'm guessing that you're not talking about alien geniuses who want to rule the universe."

"Not really."

"Then you'll have to be more specific."

"Think of somebody ruthless and glib. He'd have a lack of empathy and an inability to tell right from wrong." He pointed at the list of names. "Reminds me of Vargas."

"That's unfair. Vargas hasn't been ruthless or evil. He's been cooperative in sharing his data."

"Which he stole by hacking into my dad's computer. Come on, Eve. He's trying to manipulate you."

"How?"

"Feeding you a fancy lunch and offering those buildings for Sun Wave experiments. He's leading you on with all that talk about how you're his sister and you can ask him for anything."

"Actually, he is my half brother. According to the DNA records, we have the same mother."

"You're defending him."

"I'm focusing on the facts."

In her talks with Vargas, he'd been charming, even charismatic. She wondered if that was a behavior measured by Dr. Ray. "Did your father's paper say anything about sociopaths and charisma?"

Blake nodded. "Puller said that they were the kind of salesmen who'd promise anything to close a deal."

"That fits. Vargas knows how to say all the right words. I'm sensing that he has a hidden agenda, which is odd because I don't usually pick up on things like that. You know, motives."

He spun her around in the swivel chair and pulled her closer to the bed. "I like the way you reason things through."

"You're just pleased because I think Vargas is a jerk."

"That, too."

He slid his hands along the outside of her thighs and scooted her closer for a kiss. The light pressure of his mouth on hers was a powerful distraction, especially when he was sitting on the bed they'd torn apart.

She opened her eyes and stared at him. Looking at that perfect face would never grow tiresome.

"What do you think of my information?" he asked.

"Finding the key to interpret Dr. Ray's list of behaviors would have been more useful."

"I've got Dr. Puller working on it. The number thirty-two was familiar to him. He's checking into psychological profiling tools used by the military."

"When you talked to him about the sociopath study, did Puller say that Dr. Ray mentioned any names?"

"My dad was too discreet for that. He referred to Subject X and Subject Y. No names." With the back of his hand, he stroked her cheek. "Why do you ask?"

"Two subjects show indications of extreme behavior. One is Vargas."

"And the other is Peter Gregory," he said. "My dad wrote his initials in the margin. What else have you figured out?"

"Mostly, I've been checking the DNA evidence and trying to figure out relationships." With a sigh, she turned away from him and dragged her attention back to the facts.

"It's a patchwork family tree with five mothers and eleven fathers."

Blake picked up the pages she'd scribbled on. "Somewhere in this is a motive."

"It'd help to know the identities of the sperm and egg donors," she said.

"How would that be useful?"

"More data could flesh out the picture." And there was another reason, one she hadn't really acknowledged until she said it out loud. "And I'm curious."

She couldn't help wondering about her biological parents. Who were they? What had they done with their intelligence?

She loved the parents who raised her, and she knew they'd accept her no matter what. Mom and Dad weren't going to be thrilled when she told them she was pregnant and unmarried and didn't know the father of her child. But they wouldn't turn their backs on her.

She thought of the tiny being growing within her. This was her baby. The people she'd always called Mom and Dad were the baby's grandparents. But she couldn't help wondering.

"I'm curious, too," he said.

"I thought of checking the military database. But this was twenty-six years ago. There probably wouldn't be any results."

"And a lot of paperwork."

"We could try CODIS."

"Might as well." He took out his cell phone and paced across the bedroom to the window. "Let's give Detective Gable something to do."

She left her chair and followed him. Outside, daylight was waning, and she had a pretty good idea about how she wanted to spend the rest of the afternoon and night. She wrapped her arms around him and leaned against his back, listening to his voice as he spoke to the police detective.

Though it seemed like a contradiction, she felt comfy and excited at the same time. There was so much to learn about the emotional side of life and relationships.

Blake completed his call with a promise to send the DNA charts via e-mail to be run through CODIS.

When he turned to face her, she read passion in his smile. His dark eyes warmed her blood and sent a zing of anticipation through her body. Making love this time should be even better; she wasn't a virgin anymore.

"I think we have time." He ducked his head and kissed her quickly. "We'll make time."

She pressed against him. "Are we going somewhere?"

"We need to check out Peter Gregory." He kissed her more deeply. "Tonight is Pyro's concert."

Chapter Sixteen

Heading toward downtown Denver in the sleek armored Mercedes, Blake glanced over at Eve in the passenger seat. They'd been in the car for less than eight minutes, and she was already asleep. She'd told him that she was going to nap, tilted the seat back and…zap!

Even in repose, she was vibrant. The light from the dashboard caught on the wisps of hair that fell across her forehead. Her nose twitched. Her lips were bruised from a thousand kisses, but she was smiling like a woman who had been well satisfied from an afternoon of loving.

Blake considered himself a very lucky man to be with her.

Doubling back through traffic, he watched headlights and looked for other signs that they were being followed. No need to worry about bugs or GPS devices. Not in this car. A built-in scrambler made their movements untraceable.

He merged onto the highway and checked his G-Shock wristwatch. The Pyro concert started at ten, which gave him enough time to get there.

It was hard for him to think of Peter Gregory/Pyro as a rock star. Or a criminal mastermind. In Blake's mind, Peter had always been a brat—the only son of Lou Gregory who was a friend and coworker of his dad.

They had first met ten years ago, just after Blake's dad

had joined the group practice. The office staff, their families and friends had gathered at the Gregory home for Lou's fiftieth birthday party.

Both Blake and Peter had been fifteen, and their parents had expected them to hang out together—an intention that went bad when Peter threw a hissy fit and locked himself in his bedroom, refusing to come out. Blake remembered feeling relieved; he wasn't interested in getting friendly with a scrawny, pale-skinned, spoiled whiner who couldn't get over himself long enough to sing "Happy Birthday" to his own father.

Over the years, he and Peter had bumped into each other a half-dozen times at various family and office get-togethers. Their standard practice was to give each other a nod and find somebody else to talk with.

Blake should have looked closer at Pyro, should have recognized him as a threat.

Eve exhaled a soft little sigh and shifted position to get more comfortable in the soft leather upholstery. She'd been as surprised as he had been when they had looked up Pyro online and sampled his post-apocalyptic, techno-metal rock. His sound wasn't unusual—a hard-driving beat with a discordant keyboard refrain. The lyrics were the revelation.

His latest featured song was about "The Twenty-Four." They would rise up together, these powerful yet unknown heroes with superpowers, and they would conquer the world. All would bow before them. *Twenty-four.* No coincidence that it was the same number as the subjects in the Prentice-Jantzen study.

At Latimer's house, when they had told him about his genetic parents, Pyro had claimed to be happily astonished. *Liar!* Not only was he aware of the study but he'd given considerable thought to their supposed genetic superiority. Hell, he'd written a damn ballad to sing their praises.

Additionally, he had access to the office where Blake's father might have kept his notes. Pyro could easily have stolen the research notes or made copies.

But why would he care? As a supposed rock star, it was to his advantage to claim a weird parentage. If Pyro's psychological profile showed a tendency toward antisocial personality disorder, he'd wear that label like a badge of honor.

Exiting the highway, Blake negotiated the stop-and-go city traffic on the route to Bowman Hall on Colfax Avenue, an old redstone building that had been through many transformations since its early days as an opera house. The marquee announced, "Tonight Only. Pyro." The doors had opened, and a grungy crowd jostled each other on the sidewalk to get inside.

With a little effort, Blake figured that he and Eve could fit in with the rest of the audience. True, he had a military haircut, but he hadn't shaved in two days. Nor would Eve stand out. She was, as usual, wearing a weird T-shirt with a winged monster and the word *Jabberwocky* in Gothic script. She claimed the shirt was a tribute to Lewis Carroll, a mathematician. Oh, yeah, she'd blend right in.

But he didn't want to risk taking her into a crowd. There were too many distractions, too many chances for someone to grab her.

As he parallel-parked on a neighboring street where the old mansions had been converted to offices, she wakened. When she stretched and yawned, her arms fully extended over the dashboard. Her fingers opened wide and curled shut. She hunched her shoulders, then relaxed. When she looked at him, her eyes were bright and alert. "I'm ready."

"That was a speedy wake-up."

"Da Vinci said sleep is a waste of time. All our bodies only need a twenty-minute nap every four or five hours to stay refreshed. To tell the truth, I prefer the Einstein plan."

"What's that?"

"Eight to ten hours a night." She tugged on his sleeve. "Let's pick up our backstage passes at the box office and watch the concert."

"Not necessary." After the short online sampling, he really didn't want to subject his ears to Pyro's techno-rock wailing. "Our goal is to get Pyro alone after the show and ask him a couple of questions."

She shrugged. "If he's guilty, why would he talk to us?"

"Ego."

Surrounded by his groupies, Pyro wouldn't want to look weak by avoiding them. "In that 'Twenty-Four' song, he planned to lead the rest of us into a brilliant future. You and me? He sees us as his followers."

"Not likely."

"Maybe you're his queen."

"Even worse." She rested her hand on her belly. "What if this is Pyro's baby? Do you think it was him? That he paid Prentice to do the IVF procedure on me?"

"Doesn't fit his persona," he said. "Pyro thinks he's all-powerful and irresistible. He'd try to seduce you."

But Pyro hadn't contacted them. They'd found him. What was he up to? The rocker was playing a game, but the end goal remained a mystery. The only course of action that made sense to Blake was face-to-face confrontation.

"When we see him," Eve said, "what should we do?"

"I could beat a confession out of him."

"Seriously, Blake."

"He already lied once, pretending that he didn't know about the study. I want to know why. What else is he hiding?" He checked his watch. "Let's give him a half hour or so to get the concert rolling."

She unfastened her seat belt and leaned toward him. "Do you think Ms. Mercedes would be jealous if I kissed you?"

"This is a very sexy vehicle." He shot his seat back and pulled her onto his lap. "But you have special features that the car can't match."

As they kissed, he told himself that an effective bodyguard wouldn't allow himself to be preoccupied with romance. But he just couldn't keep his hands off his beautiful, willing partner.

THOUGH THEY STOPPED short of having sex in a car parked on a city street, the windows of the Mercedes were steamed up when Eve got out. Not exactly classy, but she felt too good to care.

Blake strode around the hood to join her on the sidewalk. In an attempt to disguise his military bearing and look like a Pyro fan, he'd allowed her to line his eyes with kohl. He'd stripped off his button-down shirt, which he tied around his waist to hide his holster. His sleeveless white T-shirt showed off his tattoo and his muscular arms. In her opinion, he was so outrageously masculine that nobody would dare question his right to be anywhere he chose.

Her Pyro fan disguise was to mess up her hair and tie a knot in her Jabberwocky shirt to make it tight across her breasts. Blake had convinced her to leave her purse in the car, but she stowed her cell phone and the stun gun in her pockets.

As they strolled along the street in the warm June night, she realized this was the closest they'd come to a date. With all the passion they'd shared, he hadn't even taken her out to dinner. "When this is over, we should go out."

"Out where?"

Apparently, the eyeliner had lowered his IQ by a solid fifty points. "To dinner and a movie. A moonlit carriage ride though the city. Dancing might be involved."

"A date." He took her hand. "I wish we had more time. I've only got a couple more weeks on leave."

After his leave was up, he'd be gone. Back to the Middle East or wherever. She didn't want to think about how sad she'd be when he left.

As they approached the box office, she noticed clumps of people standing around near the entrance. Some were smoking. Several wore black shirts with red letters that identified them as Pyro staff. How many people were needed to put on a concert like this? From the clip they'd watched online, she knew that Pyro used a lot of fireworks in his act, including an effect called the "Wall of Flame."

While Blake picked up their backstage passes, she focused on two of the Pyro staff who wore dark glasses even though it was night. The taller guy had a gold pinkie ring with an amber stone. Cleft chin. Small ears. His companion had a pug nose, big ears and a paunch around his middle.

Her eidetic memory kicked in. She knew them. They were the two men in business suits who had broken into her house. They turned away from her and went through the glass doors that led into the theater lobby. As she watched, they went through a door at the far left. It almost seemed as if they wanted her to see them.

Blake joined her and slipped her backstage pass around her neck. She looked up at him. "I saw the guys who tried to grab me at my house."

His pretense at being a laid-back Pyro fan transformed. His body tensed, ready for action. The liner around his dark eyes made him look fierce. "Where are they?"

She pointed to the interior of the lobby. "They went through that door. To the left."

"Stay with me, Eve. Behind me."

Though she hadn't noticed him pulling his weapon, the Sig Sauer was in his hand. Keeping the gun close to his side so it wasn't obvious, he moved quickly into the lobby.

At one time, this theatre might have been a rococo jewel box. Not anymore. The floor was dirty brown tile. The fancy moldings and the walls were painted black. Two sets of double doors led into the auditorium. From inside, she heard crashing drums and a wailing keyboard solo.

Nobody else was in the lobby. Apprehensive, she glanced to the left and the right. "It seemed like they wanted me to see them. This could be a trap."

When he opened the door, sound erupted. The place was packed. People were waving their arms, cheering and dancing in front of their seats and in the aisles. There was a sense of the music building toward a screaming crescendo.

Blake closed the door and stepped back. "Were they wearing staff shirts?"

"Yes."

"You might be right about a trap. We'll take a different route. They probably went backstage."

Outside, they ran around the side of the building toward the rear. At the stage door, a husky man in a Pyro staff shirt stood guard. The door was open, and an undercurrent of noise pulsated into the night.

Blake paused. He took out his cell phone. "I'm calling Detective Gable. We need backup."

Good plan. Her heart hammered inside her rib cage.

Peering toward the street, she saw a threat in every shadow. They should go back to the car, lock the doors and wait for the police to arrive.

Blake snapped his phone closed. "Gable's on the way. Should be here in fifteen minutes."

"And we'll wait for him," she said hopefully.

"These guys have gotten away from me twice. It's not going to happen again. I'll take you to the car. You can wait there."

Alone and unprotected? Even though the Mercedes had reinforced armored siding and bulletproof glass, she felt safer with him. "I'll stay with you."

"Is that a logical decision?"

Nothing she felt about him was rational, but she knew that if something bad happened to him while she was hiding in the car, she'd never forgive herself. "Let's go."

At the stage door, Blake concealed his gun and flashed their passes. They entered the backstage area.

The brilliant stage lights focused on Pyro. In the wings, it was dark. There was a lot of clutter from cables and ropes and a lot of space, both horizontal and vertical. Heavy curtains rose two stories high. Above them were catwalks. The backstage crew gathered near the curtains as though preparing to do…something important, maybe the "Wall of Flame" effect. Was Pyro reaching his finale?

Blake kept his back to the wall. "Do you see them?"

The music was so loud, she could barely hear him. "They vanished."

"We can go behind the back curtain to the other side."

"Wait."

With Blake close beside her, she went over to a guy with shoulder-length dreadlocks and showed him her backstage pass. Leaning close so he could hear her over the music, she said, "I'm looking for two guys on your staff. They always wear dark glasses."

When he nodded, his dreads bounced. He pointed toward a doorway without a door. A dim light shone from within, showing a stairwell leading down.

Blake guided her toward that light. There was nothing sexual about the way his hand rested on her waist. He was directing her. "As a general rule," he said, "it's not a good idea to ask the enemy for directions."

"At least we have a direction."

"Or we're being pointed toward an ambush."

It stood to reason that these men had also been the ones who had attacked at Blake's house with guns blazing. They were dangerous. The sensible thing was to turn back, but Blake didn't hesitate.

As they descended to the basement, she reached into her pocket and took out the stun gun. How did this thing work? She opened the safety and squeezed. Electricity arced between the two prongs on the end. It seemed too small to do serious damage.

On the bottom stair, he paused. As soon as they stepped into the open, they'd be an easy target. The music throbbed above them—not as loud down here. The beat was an echo, reminding her of the danger, heightening her fear.

Blake poked his head outside the stairwell and drew back quickly. "There's a hallway with a door."

"Okay." Why was he telling her?

"Ready?"

She repeated, "Okay."

Blake slung his arm around her waist and pulled her across the hallway at the foot of the stairs in a swift move. He twisted the handle on the door. Locked! Using his shoulder, he crashed through. They were inside a dark room.

The first thing she did was hit the light switch.

A single bare bulb illuminated a storage room, packed with boxes, old props and dusty costumes. The smell of grit and filth disgusted her.

Blake pulled her close. "I didn't get a real good look out there. Beyond this hallway, there's an open space—a big room. Not many lights. Theater junk scattered around."

"They could be hiding anywhere." Ready to pop out and open fire. "I say we wait for the police."

"We could use the backup," he agreed. "I'm guessing that this basement extends all the way under the stage to the opposite side. There must be several exits. They could escape before Gable gets here."

And he wanted to apprehend them in the worst way. She understood. These men were his best lead to finding his father's murderer. "What do we do?"

"Make them reveal their position. Draw their fire."

Her heart thudded. "You want them to shoot at us?"

"Not exactly."

Literally trusting him with her life, she said, "Tell me what to do."

Chapter Seventeen

Blake based his attack on two factors: these two hired guns weren't experienced in combat, and they were cowards. Twice before, they'd run from him. More difficult was the problem of engaging in a firefight while keeping Eve safe. He couldn't leave her in this room where she could be easily captured.

He told her to stay low, to find a hiding place in the larger room outside the hallway and to use her stun gun if anyone approached her. Any minute, Detective Gable would be here.

"Why not wait for him?" she asked.

"Gable's smart," he said. "He'll block the backstage exits. But he won't have the manpower to monitor the audience. The Pyro staff can use the crowd to escape."

"The whole staff? Do you think they're all involved?"

"Don't know. All I'm worried about right now is apprehending these two."

Grabbing junk from the prop room, he threw together a dummy target that would go ahead of them. He had to move fast, to provoke gunfire before they knew what they were shooting at.

He turned to her. "Ready?"

She nodded mutely. Her eyes were wide but not fearful.

Her bravery touched him. He would die to protect this woman.

While the music throbbed from overhead, he dashed from the hallway into the larger room. In the dim light, he saw open space, junk and shadows. With one hand, he thrust the makeshift dummy in front of them. The other hand held his gun.

A flash of gunfire showed the position of his adversaries. Straight ahead and to the left.

Blake threw the dummy to the right and ducked behind a crate. They were only ten feet from the gunmen. "Stay here," he told Eve.

He moved away from her, drawing their fire. He was close enough that he could see them when they peeked out to shoot. He returned fire. Even louder than the music, he heard a shout. One of them had been hit.

The other man took off running. The son of a bitch was going to get away. Again.

Blake couldn't pursue until he knew the first gunman was no longer a threat. He approached the place where he'd seen gunfire. The man was down. Bleeding. Unconscious.

Blake took his gun and ran across the basement. He was just in time to see the second man, the taller one, dive into the stairwell.

He followed. A narrow flight of stairs led straight up to an open doorway. He aimed both handguns in front of him, ready to blast anyone stupid enough to get in his way.

Without firing a shot, he emerged in the backstage area. Under normal circumstances, his two-gun entrance would have attracted attention. But the backstage area was busy with what had to be the climax to the concert. The lights onstage flashed and flared. Smoke machines blew a heavy mist across the floor. He caught a glimpse of Pyro breathing fire.

In an old building like this, there would be strict regulations about setting off fireworks, but the Pyro staff had come up with their spectacular special effect—the so-called wall of flame.

Blake had seen it online, but the real thing was more impressive. A shimmering, translucent curtain of red, orange and yellow strips rose slowly from the back of the stage. Lights flashed against it. A wind machine rippled the fabric. From the audience, it would look as if a wall of flames consuming the theater.

Behind his keyboard, Pyro screamed about how "The Twenty-Four" would take over the world. Blake caught sight of his quarry.

He pursued, jumping over cables on the floor and shoving people out of his way. Smoke billowed around his feet.

The area behind the scrim with rising flames allowed light to bleed through. Blake spotted the other man. Diving, he tackled his adversary, knocked him to the floor, flat on his belly. He shoved his guns into his belt and disarmed the other man. Finally, he had this guy. Finally, he'd get some answers.

The music stopped. The stage went black.

From the auditorium, the audience screamed for more.

Backstage, dim safety lights cast minimal illumination. Blake heard voices around him, felt hands pulling him off their friend. Instead of fighting one man, he was battling a mob.

He heard a shout from his left. "Police. Freeze."

A hand grasped his shoulder and pulled him back.

Blake wrenched free before he lost his grip on the gunman, but the guy had seen his chance. He struggled, put up a hell of a fight. "Back off," Blake yelled. "I'm with the cops."

His words had no effect. The rest of Pyro's staff swarmed him, dragged him off the man he had pinned on the floor. It was tempting to use the gun to clear the area, but these others might be innocent.

On his feet, Blake reacted by instinct. Using the butt of the gun, he whacked one guy in the head. Another doubled over in pain when he unleashed a hard jab to the gut.

In the shadows, he saw somebody moving to help him, pulling the attackers away from him. There wasn't enough light to see who was on his side, and Blake's only concern was to catch the gunman who attacked in the basement, to prevent him from fleeing.

The lights came back up. He saw the man fighting on his side. Vargas. His nemesis. What the hell?

Blake pointed to the gunman who was escaping. "Stop him."

And there was Eve. She jabbed her stun gun into the man's side, and he went down.

An hour later, Eve sat on the edge of the stage with her feet dangling. She'd always prided herself on being observant, but she hadn't been able to produce much in the way of useful information when questioned by Detective Gable. Too much had happened too fast. The shooting. The music. The chase. The wall of flame.

Her brain was still sorting through the details.

The aftermath was equally confusing. An ambulance raced in and picked up the man who Blake shot in the basement. He was expected to survive, thank goodness. Other paramedics treated the various people injured in the backstage brawl.

The other man—the guy Blake risked his life in

pursuing—was in custody, not talking and demanding a lawyer. Who was he? The rest of Pyro's staff claimed they didn't know. According to them, these two jerks in sunglasses had joined their crew a few hours ago. Were they all lying? Gable and the other police were still sorting out witness accounts, taking names and checking identifications.

She exhaled a sigh, and her shoulders slumped. Close to midnight, her energy was running low, and she wished she could take another Da Vinci–style power nap.

Vargas came up behind her. "Mind if I join you?"

"Suit yourself."

He sat on the edge of the stage beside her. In his jeans and denim shirt, he looked casual but still expensive. His left hand was wrapped in a bandage. "Are you all right, Eve?"

"I wasn't injured."

"You handled yourself well."

Though raised on military bases, she tended to be more of a pacifist. Not a fighter. She hadn't expected to enjoy using the stun gun, but when she had zapped the bad guy and he had gone down, she'd felt a kind of thrill.

That exhilaration was long gone, replaced by the frustrating awareness that they still had too many unanswered questions. She wanted answers, starting with Vargas. "Why are you here? At lunch, you told me that you didn't know any of the others, including Pyro."

"I saw him at the funeral. Thought I might take advantage of the concert to meet him. It was a bad idea."

She'd seen him join in the fight when Blake was struggling with the gunman. Vargas had taken his side, which meant he was an ally. Or was he? She knew better than to trust her genetic half brother. "A bad idea? Why?"

"Because Pyro has left the building." He shrugged.

"According to his staff, he always ends his concerts the same way. The big finale with smoke and flames. Then, he's gone."

"I doubt he vanished into thin air."

"The police can't reach him on the phone. Supposedly, he goes underground after a big performance. They might not hear from him for days."

In her opinion, Pyro's convenient disappearance meant he was fleeing the scene. Coupled with his connection to the two thugs who broke into her house, Pyro was beginning to look a lot like the person who had killed Blake's father. Unfortunately, circumstantial conjecture wasn't proof.

Vargas cleared his throat. "Did you get the information I e-mailed to you?"

"Yes, thank you." Her guard went up. She needed to be careful about how much she revealed. "It's difficult to decipher, but I saw that you and I share the same mother. Your father, however, is unique."

"I noticed that, too. I was the only child from that sperm donor."

An observation wasn't an answer. Tomorrow night when she finally talked to Dr. Prentice, she'd get closer to the truth. "In the psychological profile, you showed several extreme behaviors."

"My ratings were high."

So were Pyro's. "Do you have any idea what behaviors were being measured?"

"I'm aggressive," he readily admitted. "And I'd rate high in organization. I'm an effective public speaker. Also, I have musical talent and an exceptional ability with numbers."

"I wouldn't give you high marks for modesty."

"I'm confident with good reason." He grinned. "I get results."

She thought of the traits for antisocial personality disorder. "Would you call yourself ruthless?"

"I wouldn't. Others would." He reached over and patted her hand—an uninvited attention that made her want to pull away from him. "Before my twentieth birthday, I was a millionaire. What does that say about me?"

"That you're not a pussycat?"

"God, I hope not."

Blake joined them, taking a seat on her other side. Stage dirt smeared his sleeveless white T-shirt, and she noticed a couple of bruises on his bare arms. The eyeliner had left dark smudges on his face. He reminded her of a warrior, embattled and heroic.

Leaning around her, he spoke to Vargas. "I haven't had a chance to thank you. I appreciated your help."

"The least I could do," he said. "Eve was the one who really saved the day."

When they both looked at her, she was embarrassed. "Shucks, boys. It was nothing."

Vargas asked, "What have the police found out?"

"They have basic identification," Blake said. "The two thugs are from San Francisco. No current warrants, but they've both got criminal records."

"How did they get backstage?"

"The stage manager said they told him they were pyrotechnic specialists, studying the act to come up with new special effects. They flashed a bogus contract."

With his right hand, Vargas smoothed the white streak in his black hair—an unnecessary gesture because his hair wasn't out of place. She wondered what it would take to shatter his smooth façade. An accusation?

"Statistically," she said, "Dr. Ray's psychological profiles show that you and Pyro had much in common."

"Not surprising," Vargas said. "Even if we don't share the same DNA, we were designed to be high-functioning."

"Designed," Blake said with disgust. "I hate that idea."

Simultaneously, she and Vargas asked, "Why?"

She glanced over her shoulder at her genetic half brother. Knowing that she was speaking for both of them, she said, "There's nothing wrong with scientific experimentation."

"I've got nothing against science," Blake said. "But I'm not an experiment. My life is a hell of a lot more than a sperm and egg that got mixed together in a petri dish."

"That's your father's thesis," Vargas said. "He always said that upbringing and environment are more important in psychological development than genetics."

"My dad didn't get involved in this study for science. He did it for love."

She marveled at the beautiful simplicity of his reasoning. "Dr. Ray loved his wife and wanted to give her a child, even if it meant dealing with Prentice. When you were born, he loved you, too."

In his way, Dr. Ray had loved all of them, all the subjects in the study. He followed their development—year by year—with an interest that was more than statistical.

And one of them had killed him.

She turned to Vargas, determined to shake his overwhelming confidence. "You and Pyro have other similarities. You're both musically talented, both successful in your field."

"Stop right there." Vargas gestured to the auditorium that lay before them. The lights were up, showing the litter on the floor, the dirty walls and the rows of beat-up seats. "I wouldn't call a performance in this third-rate venue an example of success."

"Pyro has a following," she said. "All those screaming fans think he's a star."

Vargas scoffed. "He's a prancing moron leading others of his ilk."

"And you have something else in common," she said. "Both you and Pyro knew about the study. That's why he sings that song about the twenty-four—the superheroes who are going to take over the world. How did he find out? Do you know?"

"I don't," Vargas said. "It could be that Pyro and I are flip sides of the same coin."

Or maybe, just maybe, Vargas was lying. What was that description of sociopathic behavior? They could look you in the eye and tell you what you wanted to hear. Their idea of truth was defined by whatever was best for them.

"Here's the good news," Blake said. "Detective Gable says we're free to go."

He rose to his feet, grasped her hand and pulled her upright. Standing, she realized that her legs were a bit wobbly. In some ways, this had been the best day in her life—the day when she finally lost her virginity. In others, this twenty-four-hour period had been exhausting.

Blake smiled down at her. "Tired?"

"Oh, yeah."

"Get some rest," Vargas said. "A woman in your condition needs plenty of sleep. Don't hesitate to call me if you need anything. That goes for both of you."

Blake shook his hand. "Thanks, again."

As Vargas strode off the stage, she snuggled against Blake's chest. "Sleep sounds really good to me."

"I don't want to drive all the way back to the burbs," he said. "We'll stay in a downtown hotel tonight."

She thought of crisp sheets and chocolate mints on the pillow. "Wonderful."

Halfway down the street to the car, she was hit by an insight. "Vargas is up to something."

"I'd agree," Blake said. "Even though he took my side, I don't trust—"

"He said that a woman in my condition needed sleep."

"And?"

"I never told him I was pregnant."

Chapter Eighteen

Spray from the steaming hot shower pelted Blake's shoulders and ran down his back, soothing the minor bruises from his brawl at the theater. Staying in a downtown hotel had been the right decision; he was so tired that he might have fallen asleep at the wheel driving back to his dad's house, and it would have been a shame to wreck that beautiful Mercedes.

Random thoughts popped inside his brain. Vargas knew more than he was telling. Having him show up at the concert where the two thugs made their final play had been more than coincidence. If anyone was clever enough to be a criminal mastermind, it had to be Vargas.

But Pyro had fled the scene. A classic admission of guilt?

And what about Latimer? His contact with Prentice was damned suspicious, and he had a strong motive to suppress the information in the Prentice-Jantzen study.

One of those men had killed his father. If Blake hadn't been so tired, he might have reached out and grasped the solution.

Getting out of the shower, he dried himself off and wrapped a towel around his waist.

In the bedroom, the lights were on, and the flat-screen television showed a late-night talk show. Apparently, Eve had been trying to stay awake. Swaddled in a terry-cloth robe, she sat on top of the quilted bedspread. In her limp hand, she held the TV remote, but her eyes were closed, and her head drooped forward. She reminded him of a kid, struggling to stay up past bedtime. "Oh, Eve," he murmured, "what am I going to do about you?"

The connection between them grew deeper with every moment he spent in her presence. Truly, he thought of her as a partner. She was brave, smart and damn good-looking. Her hair, still damp from the shower, fell in blond tendrils to frame her lovely face. Gently, he kissed her forehead and took the remote from her hand.

He turned off the television. Silence filled the room. They would be safe tonight.

When he repositioned her under the covers, she murmured but didn't waken. He threw off his towel and slipped into bed beside her. Still asleep, she snuggled into his arms.

Being with Eve felt right. If she'd been awake, she would have pointed out the logical objections to why they couldn't be together. His work in Special Forces required him to travel all over the globe. She was pregnant, and the father of her baby might be the man who had killed his dad. If awake, she'd tell him that they'd only been together a couple of days and he'd get over her.

Blake knew better. He trusted his feelings more than the facts. His heart told him that Eve was the woman he wanted. She was his destiny.

He dropped into a deep, peaceful sleep.

Later that night, still in a dream state, he felt her supple, naked body resting in his arms. He caressed the curve of her slender waist, marveling at the satin texture of her skin. When he stroked the flare of her hips, she moved closer to him.

Stretching, she molded her body to his. She planted a moist kiss in the hollow of his throat. Unsure of whether he was awake or asleep, he accepted the fantasy. In the sweet, silent darkness, he made love to her.

IN THE MORNING, Blake awakened gradually, aware that he was sleeping in a strange and luxurious bed. He reached across the sheets, expecting to find Eve. She was gone.

His eyelids popped open. Where was she? Had she vanished like a dream? An irrational sense of bereavement shot through him. He didn't want to lose her, didn't want to be apart, not even for a minute.

Leaving the bed, he went to the closed bathroom door and pressed his ear against it, listening. He didn't hear water running. "Eve?"

"Oh, good. You're up. Come on in."

He pushed open the door and saw her, fully dressed and alert. She sat cross-legged on the bathroom floor with her laptop open in front of her.

He asked, "What are you doing?"

"I didn't want to turn on a light and wake you." She beamed a smile. "I was wide-awake and figured I could use this time to update a project at Sun Wave."

"You've been working?"

"Sure. With my cell phone and my computer, I can do most of my work from any location."

"Anywhere?" he asked. "Even on the other side of the planet?"

"Or from outer space." She closed her laptop and stood. "But if we're going that far, I'd like to get breakfast first."

Aware that he was naked, he retreated into the bedroom and gathered up his clothes. The glimmer of a plan took root in his mind. If all she needed for work was a computer, there was no reason why she couldn't come with him when he returned to the Middle East. Of course, he wouldn't take her into an active combat zone. But there were safe places.

While he showered again and dressed, he came up with a plan for the day. First, breakfast. Then, shopping. His clothes from last night were filthy with backstage dirt, and Eve probably felt the same way about her clothes. Maybe he could convince her to buy something more attractive than a T-shirt.

He came out of the bathroom into the large bedroom where the curtain was open. Sunlight poured through the window; it was after ten o'clock in the morning.

Eve sat at the cherrywood desk with her laptop open in front of her. He came up behind her, rested his hands on her shoulders and peeked at the computer screen, expecting to see an indecipherable array of equations. Instead, he saw typed paragraphs.

Leaning down, he kissed her cheek. "What are you working on?"

She turned her head and kissed him back. "We got a reply from Dr. Puller. He found a statistical key to decipher your dad's information. It was an old form used by the military to measure personality traits."

"This should be interesting." In the course of his military service, Blake had undergone a vast number of surveys and tests for both physical and mental ability. The results were usually annoying. He stood at the window and looked out. They were on the tenth floor and would have had a nice view of the mountains if there hadn't been another tall building in the way.

"Dr. Puller interpreted the numerical codes. He wanted to be sure we understood that this kind of statistical survey isn't an exact science. The traits indicate potential behavior rather than fact. For example, a person might have a leaning toward creativity but it doesn't mean they'll become an artist."

"What does it say about you?"

"Puller didn't know my name, of course. He only had the random numbers for identification."

He sensed that she was dancing around instead of giving him the answer. "Let's hear it, Eve. Are you a potential..." he tried to think of what would be the most incongruous fate for her—something illogical and nonscientific "... poet?"

"I wouldn't mind that at all. Poetry requires an understanding of stanza and tempo. Numbers."

"Maybe you're a potential palm reader."

"Yuck. No."

He teased, "A stripper?"

"You wish." She left the desk and joined him at the window. "I'm an introvert. No surprise there. I'm also logical and judgmental with a strong sense of right and wrong."

It didn't take a psychological profile to make that analysis. Two minutes of conversation with her would lead to the same result. "What else?"

Her wide mouth pulled into a frown. "I'm patient, nurturing and empathetic. Apparently, I have all the traits of a good mother."

She looked so disappointed that he almost laughed. "Is that a problem?"

"Well, it's convenient since I'm pregnant. But I never thought of myself that way. Me? A mom?"

He pulled her into his arms and kissed the top of her head. Puller's conclusion didn't shock him in the least. From the time he'd seen her caring for the feral cats in her alley, he'd known that she had a nurturing personality. "It's not so bad. Madame Curie was a mother."

"When I was growing up and all the other girls played with baby dolls, I never had an interest. My favorite toys were geometric. Like building blocks."

"No reason why you can't do both. Play with babies and build skyscrapers with solar panels."

She tilted her head up and grinned at him. "Now let's talk about you."

"Let me guess." He remembered all his dad's lectures. "I'm too reckless."

"Correct," she said. "You're also decisive and goal-oriented. According to Puller, once you set your mind to something, you won't rest until you've achieved it. You deal well with trauma, which is lucky considering your line of work."

He was waiting for the downside. "What else?"

"A lot of your decisions are based on emotion. As much as you're a fighter, you're a lover, too."

As soon as she spoke, he recognized an important part of himself. "That's my dad's influence."

Throughout Blake's life, his dad had shown him—through words and by example—that emotion was important. No matter what course had been charted by his genetics, his upbringing taught him to care about other people and made him a better man.

Eve rested her head on his chest. "We were lucky, you and me. We had good parents."

"What about the other subjects?"

"Problems. Nasty problems." She stepped away from his embrace and returned to the computer screen. "Latimer is selfish and demanding with a huge ego."

"What about Pyro and Vargas?"

She winced. "Both show sociopathic tendencies."

"Meaning?"

"High potential for violence."

EVE WASN'T SURE IF breakfast in the hotel coffee shop counted as a first date. Blake had invited her, chosen the place and he paid for the food. But the meal was more about expedience than enjoying each other's company.

The shopping trip that followed breakfast definitely wasn't a date. They'd gone to a trendy little boutique in Larimer Square—not the kind of place she usually shopped. Blake kept pushing her toward sexy satin things and plunging necklines. She settled on a formfitting black cashmere sweater with short sleeves. It wasn't her first choice, but she liked the way he looked at her when she was wearing it. He insisted on buying the long, belted sweater that went with it because it might get chilly later, and they didn't have time to go back to the house.

Their visit to the police station definitely wasn't a date. Nor was it useful. Detective Gable informed them that the two men in custody had lawyers and refused to say who had hired them. When it came to investigating Vargas, Gable's hands were tied. Vargas might be a raging psycho, but he was also a wealthy and powerful member of the community. Gable needed more than a psychological profile to get a warrant. Pyro was another story. The police were on the lookout for him, but he hadn't surfaced.

At six o'clock—two hours before they were scheduled to meet Prentice—Blake took her to a Mexican restaurant in west Denver. He chose the place because he thought she'd like it. And there was candlelight. When they were shown to their table, he held her chair as she sat.

"This is a date," she said.

"If you say so."

"Have you brought other women here?"

"Once or twice." He sat across the table. "None of them were as beautiful as you."

"Thank you." She'd been trained to politely accept compliments, even if they were blatant exaggerations.

"I mean it. That black cashmere sweater makes your skin glisten like a pearl."

His flattery reinforced her sense of being on a date. "Why this restaurant?"

"I know the family who owns the place. The food's great. Later on, there's a mariachi band."

"The possibility of dancing," she said. "That seals the deal. This is definitely a date."

"Courtship rituals aren't important. You know how I feel about you, Eve."

In point of fact, she didn't know. He hadn't actually stated his feelings. Though they'd made love four times, including that dreamy passion in the hotel last night, there had been no declarations. "I like going out, being wined and dined—visiting different places, seeing different views, tasting different foods."

"Do you take many vacations?"

"Not really." Usually, she used her time off to visit family. "I enjoy traveling, but making all the arrangements isn't my thing."

"I'd take care of the arrangements."

She wasn't sure what he was getting at. "It almost sounds like you're offering to sweep me away to some exotic locale."

"Have you ever wanted to see the pyramids? I know a guy who charters boat trips on the Nile."

"I'll bet you do." When they'd walked through the door of the restaurant, he was greeted like a long lost son. Blake was the kind of guy who made friends easily.

"The Middle East is incredible. Have you been there?"

"No." Her dad had been stationed in Germany when she was very young, but his other postings had been stateside.

"When my leave is up, I want to take you back with me."

That was a bit more of a date than she'd been hoping for. "You want to take me where?"

"To wherever I'm posted." He reached across the table and took her hand. His manner was calm, as though he was suggesting a walk about the park instead of a trip to the other side of the world.

She shook her head. "I can't."

"This morning, you told me that you could do your work anywhere. All you need is a computer and a cell phone."

That was true. There was a strong likelihood that she could arrange a consulting position with Sun Wave that didn't require her to be in the office. She could communicate via video feed and... Her imaginings came to an abrupt halt. *What am I thinking? I can't run off to faraway places with Blake.* She hardly knew him. "Have you forgotten that I'm pregnant?"

"Medical care isn't a problem. Some of the best hospitals in the world—"

"It's not that," she said. "When I have my baby, I want to be with family, with my mother."

"You'd be with me," he said.

Her gaze met his, and her resistance faded. Every beat of her heart said, *Go with him. Follow this perfect man to the ends of the earth.*

This isn't happening! Every decision she'd ever made was based on logic. She needed to make charts and graphs and figure the statistical probability of forming a successful relationship under these circumstances.

His cell phone rang. Without releasing her hand, he took it from his pocket and checked the screen. "It's Gable. I need to answer."

Leaning back in her chair, she stared at the flickering candle on the table, not knowing whether to laugh or cry. Nothing made sense. And yet, everything was clear.

He ended his call. "Gable finished running the DNA from all the biological parents through CODIS. He got a hit."

A momentary panic rushed through her. What if the hit was one of her parents? What if the criminal database showed that her DNA came from a felon? "Who was it?"

"Pyro." His jaw tightened. "Pyro's biological father is a convicted serial killer."

Chapter Nineteen

The match from CODIS sapped Blake's appetite. His *carne asada* burrito was made the way he liked it with the chili hot and the cheese smooth, but he could barely make a dent in his extra-large portion.

Eve had looked up information on Pyro's father using a phone app. It had taken the FBI twelve years to track this bastard down. With over forty kills in seven different states attributed to him, he was a Ted Bundy–type serial killer—charming, intelligent and grotesque in his cruelty. And they were dealing with his son.

"Just because Pyro shares his DNA," Eve said, "it doesn't mean he'll turn out the same way."

"What about the psychological profile?"

"It's not proof." Her voice was firm. "Detective Gable told you that he had no evidence against Pyro."

"Until now, he hasn't been looking. That's changed. Gable is checking Pyro's schedule for his on-the-road concerts to see if it coincides with any unsolved murders in those towns."

"It isn't right to condemn him because of his DNA." She bit into her fish taco, chewed and swallowed. Apparently, a dinner-table chat about a serial killer didn't turn her stomach. "If we start making judgments because of genetics, then—"

"We aren't talking about a scientific theory, Eve. Pyro could have killed my father. Possibly others. When he does his disappearing act after his concerts, where does he go? What does he do?"

She leaned across the table and stared into his eyes. "He's not a case study. He's Peter Gregory, and you've known him since you both were teenagers. Your father has been observing him since he was born. Do you really think Dr. Ray would have misdiagnosed a serial killer?"

She had a point. If his father thought there was a possibility of Peter doing violence to himself or anyone else, he would have contacted the police. "Do you think Prentice knew?"

"We'll find out tonight." She checked her wristwatch. "In less than an hour."

He forced himself to eat. Eve was correct. Making assumptions about Pyro based on his DNA was ignorant; it went against everything his father believed. A person's fate wasn't predestined by their genetics.

"If Pyro is the murderer," Eve said, "what's his motive?"

"If my dad's research became public, a lot of people would condemn him."

"Not his fans. He breathes fire onstage. The extra element of danger would be a plus for Pyro's concerts."

Earlier, he'd drawn much the same conclusion. The negative publicity related to having a serial killer for a father would be a problem for their other two suspects, Vargas and Latimer. Pyro wouldn't give a damn.

"Okay, let's look at his onstage performance. In his song 'The Twenty-Four,' he talks about building a heritage from the original subjects of the study. That gives him a reason to want you to be pregnant."

"Yuck. As if I'm some kind of breeder?"

"You tell me. You're the science-fiction expert."

Her brow pulled into a scowl. "It fits with the whole 'take over the world' mentality."

"The threats to you started when you suggested that you might give the baby up for adoption. Pyro might lose track of the child."

"But I only talked to Prentice."

"Who must have communicated with the murderer." Dr. Prentice had a great deal to answer for. Blake couldn't wait to get his hands on that old coward.

She finished off her food and dabbed at her lips with the corner of her napkin. "I wish we'd had time for you to give me self-defense lessons."

"You did okay with your stun gun. All you have to remember is to go for the vulnerable spots."

"Like what?"

"Eyes, nose, gut, groin, knees. And you have to hit hard. Don't hold back."

This meal—their first real date, according to Eve—had started well. When he proposed taking her with him, she'd warmed to the idea. Though she'd objected, he'd seen acceptance in her eyes, and he'd allowed himself to imagine a future with her. For a moment, he'd managed to push the tragedy of his father's murder from his mind.

The call from Gable re-tuned his focus. Mentally, he dedicated himself to finding the killer and bringing him to justice.

DURING THE DRIVE to Latimer's office, Eve couldn't stop thinking about floating down the Nile with Blake, sharing his life in exotic places. She'd been tempted to take that leap, to throw away her life as a singular individual and join him.

In the lights from the dashboard, she studied his profile.

His straight nose was so perfect that he should have been on a coin. Was it possible that a man like Blake wanted to live with her? In a few short days, how could he care so much? The word *love* hadn't passed his lips. Nor had she made that declaration.

Though inexperienced in matters of the heart, she figured there should be a commitment before she abandoned her life in Boulder and followed him to the ends of the earth. Did he love her?

She had to know.

"Earlier tonight," she said, "you told me that you wanted me to come along when you returned to active duty."

"That's right." He braked for a stoplight and turned toward her. "We'll talk later. I need to maintain focus on the task at hand."

"I just have one question."

And she knew the answer she needed to hear: *Because I love you.* That was all he had to say. If he loved her, she could acknowledge all the strange and wonderful feelings that stirred when she looked at him or thought of him or heard his voice. She needed to know if he loved her.

"Okay," he said. "Shoot."

"Why? What is the single most important reason you want to take me with you?"

"I told you before," he said. "My dad's last wish was that I take care of you."

Of all the things he could have said, that might have been the most insulting. He made it sound as if she was an obligation, a burden. The hell with him. "You're officially off the hook, Blake. I can take care of myself."

"We'll talk about this later."

There were so many other things he could have said. He could have told her that he wanted her with him because she was sexy. Or because she was different from the other women he'd known. He could have told her that he couldn't live without her.

But his offer didn't have anything to do with her. Being her bodyguard was a job. "There's no need for discussion."

Her mind was made up. Thank God, she hadn't started packing her bags and making plans. She hadn't made a complete fool of herself.

"Eve, please—"

"No talking." She held up her hand. "Let's just get this over with."

The Mercedes glided into the parking lot outside Latimer's three-story office building. The last crimson rays of sunset reflected in the rows of windows and gave the square building a more interesting appearance than when they'd been here at night. Vargas's building, she remembered. Would he designate this structure as one that could be converted to solar energy? She looked away, not really caring. Her future felt bleak. She'd be alone. Pregnant. *At least, I'm not a virgin anymore.*

Blake parked beside the Cadillac sedan that Randall used to chauffeur his boss. He peered through the windshield. "Where's Prentice's car?"

"He could be running late."

"I don't like the way this looks," he said. "Call Latimer. Find out where Prentice is."

"Yes, sir." She snapped a sarcastic salute. He was always giving orders, making demands. Why had she vaguely considered living with him? Her call to Latimer went straight to voice mail. "He's not answering."

He pulled his gun. "Let's check it out."

Remembering what she'd done at the theater, she left her purse behind, slipping her cell phone in one pocket and the stun gun in another.

As they approached the glass doors at the front of the building, she reminded him, "Latimer's office is on the third floor."

"I know. I was here with you the other night."

"Just trying to be helpful."

She couldn't wait until this so-called investigation was finished. They'd talk to Prentice, find out the name of the murderer and call Detective Gable to make the arrest. Then she could say goodbye to Blake. He'd stride off into his perfectly handsome world, and she'd go back to...being herself.

Her fingers stroked the edge of the long cashmere sweater he had insisted on buying for her. She wasn't meant to wear clothes like this. A Trekkie T-shirt suited her just fine—an extra-large to fit her when she was in the last stages of pregnancy.

The doors at the front pushed open. In a small office building like this, there was no guard at a front desk. The polished floors at the front led to two elevators.

She heard the pop of gunfire. "Damn."

Blake pulled her into the stairwell. "Stay with me. Just like you did at the theater."

Assuming there was some tactical reason why they couldn't use the elevator, she followed him up three flights of stairs. The gunfire continued in sporadic bursts.

When they reached the third floor, Blake positioned her behind the door. Breathing hard, she pressed her back against the concrete wall. Before he could deliver his order, she said, "I know. I should stay. Right here."

He whipped open the door and dashed through.

Trembling, she waited, holding her stun gun. Fear built up inside her. The internal pressure was unbearable. To calm herself, she counted prime numbers. Her brain stumbled and stuck on twenty-five. *Not a prime.* Why was she thinking of twenty-five? It was her age. Blake's age. They should have more years. Together? *No, we won't be together.*

Her usually organized mind bounced wildly from one thought to the next. She was confused, horribly confused. Her hands rose to her temples as though she could control her brain by holding the sides of her head. If she stood here by herself, she'd surely go mad.

With her stun gun in hand, she opened the door and peeked into the well-lit hallway. The elevators stood in the center of the third floor. At either end the hallways took a ninety-degree turn, creating a square within the square building. The hall was clean and plain with one exception: blood stained the carpet and splattered on the clean white walls.

A single shot rang out. She didn't see the gunman. Or Blake. Or anyone else. Only the blood.

She went around the corner to the left. The door to Latimer's office stood open.

She glanced over her shoulder toward the stairwell. If she went back, she'd be safe from stray bullets. But safety was relative. If someone attacked her in the stairwell, she couldn't escape. In the theater when Blake had taken off in pursuit of the bad guy, she'd made a reasoned decision to follow him. The safest place she could be was close to him.

Ducking low, she darted toward the open door. Blake was inside, crouched behind the receptionist's desk in the waiting room where a row of slate-blue chairs lined the walls and magazines rested on a coffee table. Smears of blood marked the floor, leaving a trail.

Blake called out, "Damn it, Latimer. Put down the gun."

"Stay back." Latimer's voice was high and scared. "You can't take this from me. I won't let you."

In the narrow corridor that led to the examination rooms, she caught a glimpse of Latimer. He lurched forward, fired wildly and stumbled back. He wasn't wearing his glasses, which meant he was nearly blind. And armed.

She scooted across the floor to Blake's side. He pulled her close. "I was starting to worry about you. I'm glad you're here."

An unwanted thrill went through her. She nodded toward the hallway. "What's happening?"

"As near as I can figure, Latimer has lost his damn mind. He thinks I'm after him."

"The blood?"

"I don't know. I haven't seen anybody else."

From down the hall came another desperate shout. "I know you're there. Don't come any closer."

She looked to Blake. "Have you tried getting closer?"

"I don't have a death wish," he said. "And I don't want to shoot him."

"Maybe you could throw something. You were pretty accurate with that knife in the kitchen."

Latimer fired another wild shot.

"The problem," Blake said, "is that I can't stand up and take aim."

"Maybe I should try talking to him."

"Go for it. A woman's voice might reassure him."

She faced the narrow hallway but stayed behind the desk. "Dr. Latimer? Trevor Latimer? It's me, Eve Weathers."

"Eve?"

"That's right." Her mouth felt dry. She licked her lips and forced herself to swallow. "I'm here with Blake, and we're not going to hurt you."

"Show yourself."

Before she could stand up, Blake caught her arm. "Keep him talking. Get him to disarm himself."

"Trevor," she said, "you invited me here. Remember? You said you were setting up a meeting with Dr. Prentice. Do you remember that?"

"Of course, I remember."

"I want to help you. But you have to put the gun down first. Toss it into the hallway."

"Then I'd be helpless. No."

"Please, Trevor. We're on your side. Please trust me."

"No," he shouted. "Where the hell is Randall?"

She'd forgotten all about Latimer's chauffeur and bodyguard. To Blake, she whispered, "Have you seen him?"

"When I came onto the floor, I made a circuit of the hallways, but that doesn't mean he's not hiding out there."

She eyed the blood. "Or he was shot."

Calling out to Latimer, she said, "When did you last see Randall?"

"He came with me into the building. While I was in my office, I heard shooting. Got my gun from the safe. And the ammo. Then I stumbled. Lost my glasses." His voice was growing weaker. "They can't have it. They can't take it from me."

"Take what?" she asked. What was so important that he'd protect it with his life?

"Can't take it." He fired another shot.

Unreasonable and panicked, he was hanging on to his sanity by a thin strand. Somehow, she had to get through to him. "There's a lot of blood out here. Somebody has been wounded, seriously wounded. And you're a doctor. You can help them."

"Is it Randall? Is he hurt?"

"Throw down your gun, and we'll look for Randall. We need your help."

There was silence, and she hoped that she'd reached him.

In a dull voice, Latimer said, "All right, I'll help in any way that I can."

Both she and Blake peered over the edge of the desktop as Latimer stepped into the narrow hallway and dropped his weapon.

Blake hurried to pick up the gun. She went to Latimer. She would have embraced him, but he was holding a metal container that looked like a big thermos in front of him.

Gently, she patted his arm. "What's in there?"

"Frozen sperm. Mine. It's my only chance of having a child." He exhaled a ragged breath and sagged against the wall as though he wasn't strong enough to stand on his own. "My illness left me sterile."

"I'm so sorry."

"If it weren't for Dr. Prentice, I wouldn't even have this small amount of viable sperm."

"What do you mean?" she asked.

"He took a sperm sample from me as a part of the Prentice-Jantzen study. I assume he did the same with all the subjects."

"All of you?" Even Blake? She'd have to ask him about Prentice's physical exams.

"Eight months ago, I was fine. And now…"

She couldn't help feeling empathy for this man, her own age, who had suffered the terrible ravages of disease. At the same time, her rational mind told her that his sterility was an obvious reason he might have wanted to impregnate her. He knew how such things worked; he was a fertility specialist. The most damning evidence of all: Latimer was in touch with Prentice.

"Was it you?" she asked. "Am I carrying your baby?"

"What?" He squinted, trying to see her. "What are you talking about?"

"The first time you saw me, you knew I was pregnant."

"I made an educated guess. This is what I do for a living, Eve. I help women get pregnant. I know the signs."

"Like glowing? You don't really expect me to believe that." She leaned closer, hoping that he could see her anger.

"All right," he said angrily. "Dr. Prentice mentioned that a woman close to Blake was pregnant. And you walked into my house with your hand resting on your belly."

"You'd been talking to Prentice."

"Occasionally."

"Where is he? You promised that he'd be here."

He drew away from her. "I was supposed to call him after you arrived. If you want to talk to him, use the cell phone on my desk."

Blake turned on the light in one of the examination rooms and cursed. "Over here, Latimer."

Collapsed on the floor beside the padded examination table with stirrups was Randall. His chest was covered with blood.

Chapter Twenty

While Blake and Latimer worked on Randall, Eve slipped out of the examination room. They'd called 911. Soon the parking lot outside would be filled with ambulances and police cruisers. The office would be crawling with cops.

Before she'd gotten involved with Blake, her only contact with the police was the occasional speeding ticket. Now, she knew the drill. There would be questions, confusion and a total lack of privacy.

Latimer had told her that the cell phone on his desk would connect with Prentice. She needed to make that call before the chaos descended.

Blake poked his head out of the exam room. "Eve, go out to the hallway so you can direct the paramedics. Randall needs a hospital. Every minute counts."

"I'm on it."

Before she went to the outer door, she dashed into Latimer's private office and grabbed the cell phone.

In the bloodstained hallway, she paced in front of the elevators. Prentice had the answer to her burning question: who was her baby's father?

Though she wanted to scream at him and make demands, she knew better. Prentice wouldn't respond to threats—not from her, anyway. If ever in her life she needed to be calm and rational, this was the moment. She had to convince him to tell her the truth.

She scrolled through the list of Latimer's contacts until she found the number, and she made the call.

Prentice grumbled, "It's about time, Latimer. I expected to hear from you ten minutes ago."

"It's Eve Weathers. Don't hang up."

Impatiently, he snapped, "What is it, Eve?"

"We obtained your initial research and Dr. Ray's analysis. I've deciphered most of the DNA database."

"Good for you."

His cold, sardonic tone irritated her. She lashed out. "You were careless, Doctor. You recruited a serial killer as one of the sperm donors."

"My selection process was based on IQ tests, accomplishments and health. Unfortunately, he qualified."

"Thank God, he was only the father of two subjects."

"Three," he corrected her.

"I read the DNA charts, Dr. Prentice. There was Pyro and one other man."

"You're not as clever as you think, Eve. From what source did you obtain these charts?"

"From Vargas." She had trusted the information from her genetic half brother. A mistake? "Vargas was the only subject with a unique sperm donor."

"Because he made it up," Prentice said. "David Vargas has the same genetic father as Pyro."

The serial killer. If that information was made public, Vargas would be profoundly embarrassed. In his business dealings, reputation was everything. He couldn't afford to be the son of an infamous serial killer.

Her mind took the next logical leap. "Please don't tell me that Vargas is the father of my baby."

"Certainly not. You share the same mother."

"But he's the one who paid you, isn't he? He wanted me to be pregnant."

"Because you share the same mother," Prentice said. "Vargas wanted a child that shared his DNA—the good DNA. You or your half sister could provide him with a legacy."

"That's crazy. Why wouldn't he use his own sperm? Or hire a surrogate mother to carry his baby?"

"He wanted to eliminate the DNA from his biological father, the serial killer. You share half his DNA—the good half. And he made a logical and compelling argument. You've met him, Eve. He's very convincing. I had assumed that once you knew you were pregnant, you'd come around. According to Dr. Ray's psychological analysis, you'll make an outstanding mother."

"But Dr. Ray wouldn't go along with the plan. Vargas had to kill him to keep him quiet."

Prentice rushed to say, "There's no evidence to that accusation."

"But we both know it's true. That's why you went into hiding, taking a supposed vacation. You're afraid of Vargas."

"I advise you to make the best of this situation. Think of the advantages. Vargas has enough money to provide your child with a top-notch lifestyle, an excellent education."

"It takes more than money to make a father. It takes love." She heard herself echoing Blake's words.

"We can work this out. We'll draw up contracts."

She couldn't believe he was advising her to work with the man who had probably killed Blake's father, the son of the most infamous serial killer since Jack the Ripper. "I'd rather sign a deal with the devil."

"Because you don't have all the data. There's one more important bit of—"

The cell phone was torn from her hand. She'd been so engrossed in her conversation that she hadn't heard anyone approach. He grabbed her around the torso. His other hand covered her mouth.

"Come quietly." She recognized Pyro's voice. "I won't kill you, Eve, but I can hurt you a lot."

He dragged her backward toward the stairwell. One arm was pinned to her side, but she struggled with the other. Kicked back with her legs.

"Fine," he muttered. "We'll do this your way."

He pressed a cloth over her mouth. The sharp tang of a chemical compound prickled her nostrils. She tried not to breathe but couldn't help inhaling.

The fight went out of her. Thought drained from her mind as she lost consciousness.

As SOON AS THE PARAMEDICS arrived, Blake stepped out of the way. With Latimer's help, he'd done everything he could to keep Randall alive, from rudimentary first aid to starting an IV line. The chauffeur had lost a lot of blood, and there was internal damage, but he was still breathing.

In the front waiting room, Blake turned to Latimer. "Randall's going to make it. He's a fighter."

"Thanks to you. I mean that sincerely. Thank you."

"Hey, I just did what you told me. You're the doctor. You saved him."

Latimer straightened his spine. His eyelids tensed and twitched, but he appeared to have regained his self-control. "I apologize for what happened earlier. I haven't been myself. Not since you told me about my biological parents."

Two uniformed cops entered and rushed toward the examining room. Blake looked past them to the outer hallway. He didn't see Eve.

Latimer continued, "I've been so absorbed in my own problems that I forgot that I could help others. That's why I became a doctor. Working with you to save Randall showed me that I can still contribute. I'm not dead, yet."

"Good for you." This was an important moment for Latimer, and Blake would have paid more attention, but he was beginning to worry. "Do you know where Eve went?"

"The last time I saw her was when I told her that she could contact Prentice using my cell phone on my desk."

"Where's your office?"

"Straight back and to the right."

"Thanks." Blake clapped his shoulder and dodged past the two cops blocking the narrow hallway.

In Latimer's office, he searched for the cell phone. It was nowhere in sight. He saw no sign of Eve.

Had she gone down to the car? He looked out the window into the gray light of dusk. Two more police cars pulled into the parking lot with lights flashing. *Damn it, Eve. Where are you?* He knew she was angry; she'd made it crystal clear that he'd said the wrong thing. Instead of telling her that he cared about her, maybe even loved her, he'd talked about his duty to honor his father's last wish. Not the smartest comment he'd ever made, but he had had too much on his mind to be sensitive.

And she hadn't given him a chance, hadn't given him time to explain. Was she mad enough to go storming off by herself? He didn't think so. There was still a threat, and Eve knew to be careful. Where the hell was she?

Avoiding questions from the officers who wanted to take his statement, he made his way into the hallway outside Latimer's waiting room. He'd told her to come out here and direct traffic when the cops and paramedics started to show up. What if someone had been waiting? What if he'd directed her into an ambush?

Near the stairwell, he found the cell phone. By some miracle, it hadn't been trampled. He hit redial and held it to his ear.

A voice answered immediately, "Eve? What happened?"

"Who's this?" Blake asked.

"Dr. Edgar Prentice. To whom am I speaking?"

He wanted to crawl through the phone and strangle the old bastard. "This is Blake Jantzen."

"Are you with Eve? Is she all right?"

"Why wouldn't she be?"

"I'm not sure what happened," Prentice said. "We were having a conversation, and she was interrupted. It was sudden. I fear someone might have…taken her."

"Someone," he said coldly. "You know who it was. You've known all along who was after her."

"In point of fact, I can't be sure. I don't have actual physical evidence."

"Don't waste my time playing games, Prentice."

"This can't come back to me," he said nervously. "My practice is already on shaky ground and I—"

"Stop! No more excuses! You'll start cooperating now. You have no other choice."

"I don't?"

"If anything happens to Eve, if she's harmed in any way, you'll have a reason to be scared. Because I will hunt you down." He paused to let his threat sink in. "Where would they take her?"

There was a moment of silence. The paramedics came into the hallway with Randall on a collapsible gurney. Another set of cops emerged from the elevator.

Finally, Prentice said, "There's a private airstrip in the

mountains between Boulder and Nederland. I believe it's called V-Base."

"And the *V* stands for Vargas." Blake had known from the first time he met Vargas that he was trouble.

"Be careful when you're approaching. It's my understanding that Pyro likes to play with explosives."

Both Vargas and Pyro? And a minefield? Things just kept getting more and more complicated. "What else can you tell me?"

"There's one last thing you should know. It's extremely important."

Chapter Twenty-One

Slowly, painfully, Eve became conscious. The inside of her head felt as if it was going to explode. Her limbs were stiff and cold. Her mouth tasted as if she'd been sucking on cotton balls. She licked her lips. God, she was thirsty. She pried her eyelids open.

Her wrists and ankles were bound with rope. She was huddled on a couple of blankets inside what seemed to be a barn. The only light came from a couple of hanging bulbs. One wall was completely open. The air smelled of machinery and grease.

Looking through the door into the moonlit night, she saw a long, flat stretch of land that had been cleared except for occasional clumps of persistent weeds. An airstrip. This wasn't a barn; it was an empty hangar.

Ignoring the throbbing inside her head, she struggled to sit up. Since her hands were tied in front of her, she might be able to unfasten the ropes at her ankles. She bent her legs to the side and twisted around. With numb fingers, she attacked the knots.

Outside the open door, she saw the shadows of evergreens rising on hillsides, and she heard the silence of the mountains. How far had they gone? She turned her wrist and checked her watch. It was only ten o'clock—not enough time to make a long drive. They were still fairly close to Denver. As if that made a difference? Disappearing in the vastness of the mountains was easy, and she knew it'd take a miracle for Blake to find her. He was smart and clever and had access to sophisticated technology, but he wouldn't know where to look. She might never see him again. A sob climbed up her throat. With an effort, she suppressed the sound.

She couldn't rely on Blake to rescue her. She had to do it by herself.

Her shoulders ached from the uncomfortable stretch as she fought with the ropes, but it was worth it. The knots loosened. Pyro hadn't done a real good job of tying her legs. She'd been surprised to see him, especially after what Prentice had told her. Vargas was the real villain.

With a final kick, the ropes around her ankles came off. She struggled to her feet. Standing intensified her headache. What had she inhaled that made her pass out? Chloroform? When she turned her head, the world went spinning.

She had to escape. The airstrip meant a plane was coming. She could be flown to any location, locked up until she delivered the baby. Then what? After she gave birth to the Vargas heir, she was expendable.

Staggering a few steps, she stumbled and fell hard onto the packed earth floor. Her legs were so stiff that it felt as if her bones had cracked.

"Eve!" Pyro bellowed. "I see you, Eve."

She forced herself to her feet. She wanted to run but only managed a few clumsy strides before he caught hold of her arm. Weakly, she said, "Let me go."

"Can't do that. You could be hurt bad. Exploded into a million pieces."

A surge of anger gave her strength. "What the hell are you talking about?"

"Come along," he said. "I'll show you."

As he dragged her onto the airstrip, the chill night air hit her face, and she revived a bit more. Concentrating hard, she focused on Pyro. His spiked black hair contrasted with his pale, moonlit face. With all his piercings and silver jewelry, he looked like a combination rocker and vampire. If she could get a clear shot at him, she'd smash that nose ring all the way into the frontal lobe of his sick brain.

She stumbled along beside him. "Why are you doing this?"

"You said your friend was a fan. You know my music. I thought you'd understand 'The Twenty-Four.' We have a destiny. We're the future. Why don't you get it? Aren't you supposed to be smart?"

Way too smart to follow his delusional thinking, but she wanted him to keep talking until she figured out a way to break free. "When did you find out about your genetic background?"

"If you paid attention to my songs, you'd know. I gave the date, almost a year ago, when Vargas approached me." He yanked her along with him. They were almost in the middle of the airstrip. "It's a revelation. A revolution."

"What does Vargas want you to do?"

"I'm a rock star. That makes me the front man. I'll draw people to our cause, build an army."

"And Vargas foots the bill."

"Oh, yeah, he's the money man. He's setting up record deals, hired a publicist."

"And the two guys who came after me at my house? Did Vargas hire them, too?"

"Yeah, I guess. The Big V works in mysterious ways."

She knew that Pyro had been duped, blinded by the promise of fame. He saw himself as a noble warrior, a leader. And he didn't recognize the downside. "Did Vargas tell you the identity of your biological father?"

Pyro threw back his head and laughed. Though he wasn't a big man, his gestures were larger than life. "I know he's a genius. Outsmarted the FBI for years."

"He's a serial killer."

"I've been working on a song about him. One of those 'sins of the father' things. When I start doing interviews, my DNA is going to make me special."

The idea of using a serial killer father as a publicity ruse disgusted her. Did he really believe he'd get away with this? Though they were the same age, he seemed a lot younger. Like a kid caught up in a dark fantasy game, he couldn't see reality. "Are you like your father? Have you committed murder?"

"You're talking about Dr. Ray's murder." He scowled as dramatically as a mask of tragedy. "I wouldn't hurt him. I liked him. He used to let me play his piano."

Though he'd lied to her before, she wanted to believe that he wasn't all bad. There might still be a spark of humanity in him. "What about the shoot-out at Latimer's office?"

"I was there."

But did he shoot Randall? Was he too disconnected to understand what she was asking?

He shook his head. "Too bad about Latimer. He's sick, real sick." In his right hand, Pyro held a small plastic device. "Watch this."

He pointed and pressed a button.

At the edge of the airstrip, an explosion erupted. Dirt, rocks and weeds spewed into the air in a burst of orange flame.

Stunned, she stared as the flame quickly died, leaving a smoke trail. Her ears rang with the noise.

Pointing with both fingers, Pyro turned in a circle. "I've got bombs all around. I can detonate using a remote. And they're motion-sensitive. Step on one and you're dead."

"Why?" she asked.

"Go ahead and run, Eve. If you're feeling lucky."

"Why the hell would you do this?"

"It's Pyro's wall of flame. For real." His hands rose above his head as though he'd reached the climax in one of his concerts. Then, his arms dropped.

He shrugged and gave her a boyish grin. He almost looked innocent. "I like things that go boom. Always have. Good old Dr. Ray used to worry about me setting fires."

Dr. Ray had been right to worry.

BLAKE WATCHED THE LAST wisp of smoke from the explosion curl above the treetops and disappear into the night sky. During his tours of duty, he'd had enough experience with improvised explosive devices to know they were, above all, unpredictable. He might choose a safe approach to the airstrip or, just as likely, he'd step on a trigger that would detonate another bomb.

He had to believe that Pyro brought Eve here to wait for Vargas, who would probably arrive in a small plane. Blake wouldn't let her be taken away from him. Eve was the woman he loved. And the mother of his child.

Prentice had been smug when he had told Blake that Vargas selected him as the sperm donor to be matched with her egg. His rationale was that Eve had the brains, and Blake had the brawn. They'd make a perfect match for the next generation.

Though he didn't agree with their logic or their procedure, he was overwhelmed by an amazing sense of fulfillment. This was his destiny. To be a father. Even better, Eve was the mother of his child.

He'd never believed in fate, but his love for her seemed preordained. They were meant to be together, to raise a family together. He couldn't wait to see her face when he told her, which meant he'd better get his butt in gear.

Using the GPS in his Mercedes, he'd found this location. For the past ten minutes, he'd been scouting the perimeter, keeping an eye on Pyro. For a while, he considered using a sniper rifle from his arsenal in the trunk to take Pyro out. If this had been a hostage situation in a war zone, that was how he'd handle the situation. But Blake didn't know if Pyro was guilty, and he didn't have the right to play executioner.

If he wounded Pyro from a distance, he wouldn't be close enough to prevent the rocker from taking revenge on Eve. Blake needed to get onto that airstrip.

Moving silently through the forest, he returned to the one-lane dirt road where he'd parked the Mercedes. Wistfully, he patted the sleek midnight-blue fender of the armored car. "I'm sorry, baby. You have to make the ultimate sacrifice."

Behind his back, Pyro had turned on the lights to illuminate the field. It was a short runway. Vargas must be flying a single-engine prop plane. As if to confirm that conclusion, he heard the hum of an approaching aircraft.

Blake armed himself. He kept the Sig Sauer as a handgun, clipped another holster to his belt, slung an M16 across his shoulders and moved his knife sheath to the back of his belt for easy access. Then he started the car.

It seriously pained him to damage this fine vehicle, but heading straight down the dirt road was the fastest approach.

He saw the single-engine Cessna touch down.

Pyro, holding Eve's arm, walked toward the plane.

There wasn't a minute to spare.

Still hidden in the trees, Blake gunned the engine. The road sloped down to the airstrip, and he hoped there would be enough momentum to carry the car forward. He pointed the car straight down and took off. As soon as he was out of the trees, he jumped from the driver's seat.

The Mercedes rolled down the hill, unscathed for several yards. At the edge of the airfield, the Mercedes hit the IED. The explosion was strong enough to stop the vehicle and tear off the front fender. If Blake had stepped on that bomb, he would have been toast. But the armored car weighed thousands of pounds, enough to keep her from flipping onto her side.

Though Blake had intended to run down the path cleared by the car, he saw a better way. Keeping his footprints in the tire tracks to avoid any other bombs, he got behind the wheel. He turned the key. The Mercedes started. Damn, this was one hell of a fine car.

He drove onto the airstrip.

As soon as Eve saw the Mercedes, she took heart. Blake was coming for her.

Taking advantage of Pyro's momentary astonishment as he stared at the approaching vehicle, she drew back with both hands—still tied together at the wrist—and swung as hard as she could.

When she hit him directly on the nose, he let out a scream and fell to his knees. Remembering Blake's quick lesson on self-defense, she kicked him in the crotch.

Pyro keeled over backward, curled into a ball.

She aimed another hard kick at his lower back, then another to his head. He was unconscious. She took the gun from his hand, but she couldn't hold on. Her fingers wouldn't grip.

Looking up, she saw Blake leap from the Mercedes.

Vargas was faster. She hadn't seen him emerge from the plane, but he was beside her. He pulled her in front of himself, using her as a shield. His gun pressed against the side of her head.

He yelled to Blake, "Not another step. This is a hair trigger."

She saw Blake halt. He was fifteen feet away, close enough that she could see the strength and determination on his face but too far for him to attack. He held the Sig in both hands, ready to shoot.

In a low, dangerous voice, he said, "You won't kill her. You want her baby."

"I'll make that sacrifice. Throw down your weapons."

Vargas held her so tightly that she couldn't struggle, could barely breathe.

Blake took a step closer.

The muzzle of the gun pressed harder against her skull. She didn't want to die.

"Here's my deal," Vargas said. "Throw down your weapons, and Eve will live. I'll take care of her and the baby."

All she could hear was the unspoken conclusion. If Blake disarmed himself, he'd be killed before her eyes. "Don't do it," she shouted. "Shoot him."

"He won't risk your life," Vargas said. "Blake's a hero. An honorable man. He wouldn't be able to live with the guilt if he was responsible for your death. Isn't that right, Blake?"

Without a word, Blake unfastened the holster on his belt. He reached over his shoulder and divested himself of the M16 rifle. Holding out his hand, he dropped the Sig Sauer.

Vargas shoved her to the ground. He raised his gun and pointed it at Blake. "I win."

"You won't get away with this," Blake said.

"I knew you were weak. Like your father. He died holding a photo of you and your mother."

Blake moved so fast that she couldn't describe his motions. She only saw the aftermath. His knife was buried to the hilt in Vargas's chest. He gasped. A look of horror and shock distorted his features. Still, he tried to aim his gun.

She saw Blake running toward them, but she was closer. She lunged, hit Vargas on the shoulder. He went down.

Blake grabbed his weapon. He leaned over Vargas, felt for a pulse, then shook his head. "He's dead."

She'd never seen a man die before, but all she felt was relief. They were safe. Finally, safe.

Blake knelt beside her and unfastened the ropes on her hands. "Are you all right?"

"I've been better."

Gently, he surrounded her with a warm embrace. Her arms were too weak to do more than drape around him, but she returned his kiss.

"I have something to tell you." He looked around the airstrip with the battered Mercedes at one side and the Cessna on the other. Vargas lay dead. Pyro hadn't recovered consciousness. "This doesn't seem like the right place."

"Seems to me that you'd be comfortable on a battlefield."

"I talked to Prentice, and he told me the name of your baby's father."

She braced herself for bad news. "Tell me."

A wide grin spread across his face.

"You?" She couldn't have been more shocked.

"My sperm. Your egg. We're going to have a kid."

Never again would she be a singular person, and the change in her life was more wonderful than she ever could have imagined. She and Blake would be parents. "For the next kid, let's do it the old-fashioned way."

He hugged her hard, making her a part of him. Then he lifted her to her feet. His gaze rested lightly upon her as he brushed the dirt from her shoulder. "You pretty much destroyed that nice sweater."

"Some women aren't meant to wear cashmere." She pressed against him. "Some women are meant to float down the Nile on a chartered boat."

"Does that mean you're coming with me?"

"Because I love you," she said.

"And I love you, Eve. With all my heart."

* * * * *

SPECIAL DELIVERY BABIES
concludes next month with
HOOK, LINE AND SHOTGUN BRIDE,
only from Cassie Miles.
Look for it wherever
Harlequin Intrigue books are sold!

COMING NEXT MONTH

Available September 14, 2010

HARLEQUIN®

A *Romance*

FOR EVERY MOOD™

Spotlight on

— **Heart & Home** —

Heartwarming romances
where love can happen
right when you least expect it.

See the next page to enjoy a sneak peek
from Harlequin Superromance®,
a Heart and Home series.

*Enjoy a sneak peek at fan favorite Molly O'Keefe's
Harlequin Superromance miniseries,*
THE NOTORIOUS O'NEILLS, *with*
TYLER O'NEILL'S REDEMPTION,
*available September 2010
only from Harlequin Superromance.*

Police chief Juliette Tremblant recognized the shape of the
man strolling down the street—in as calm and leisurely
fashion as if it were the middle of the day rather than
midnight. She slowed her car, convinced her eyes were
playing tricks on her. It had been a long time since Tyler
O'Neill had been seen in this town.

As she pulled to a stop at the curb, he turned toward her,
and her heart about stopped.

"What the hell are you doing here, Tyler?"

"Well, if it isn't Juliette Tremblant." He made his way
over to her, then leaned down so he could look her in the
eye. He was close enough to touch.

Juliette was not, repeat, *not* going to touch Tyler O'Neill.
Not with her fingers. Not with a ten-foot pole. There would
be no touching. Which was too bad, since it was the only
way she was ever going to convince herself the man standing
in front of her—as rumpled and heart-stoppingly handsome
now as he'd been at sixteen—was real.

And not a figment of all her furious revenge dreams.

"What are you doing back in Bonne Terre?" she asked.

"The manor is sitting empty," Tyler said and shrugged,
as though his arriving out of the blue after ten years was
casual. "Seems like someone should be watching over the
family home."

"You?" She laughed at the very notion of him being here
for any unselfish reason. "Please."

HSREXP0910

He stared at her for a second, then smiled. Her heart fluttered against her chest—a small mechanical bird powered by that smile.

"You're right." But that cryptic comment was all he offered.

Juliette bit her lip against the other questions.

Why did you go?

Why didn't you write? Call?

What did I do?

But what would be the point? Ten years of silence were all the answer she really needed.

She had sworn off feeling anything for this man long ago. Yet one look at him and all the old hurt and rage resurfaced as though they'd been waiting for the chance. That made her mad.

She put the car in gear, determined not to waste another minute thinking about Tyler O'Neill. "Have a good night, Tyler," she said, liking all the cool "go screw yourself" she managed to fit into those words.

It seems Juliette has an old score to settle with Tyler.
Pick up TYLER O'NEILL'S REDEMPTION
to see how he makes it up to her.
Available September 2010,
only from Harlequin Superromance.

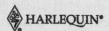

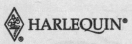
HARLEQUIN®

American ★ Romance®

TANYA MICHAELS
Texas Baby

Babies
&
Bachelors
USA

Instant parenthood is turning Addie Caine's life
upside down. Caring for her young nephew and
infant niece is rewarding—but exhausting! So when
a gorgeous man named Giff Baker starts a short-term
assignment at her office, Addie knows there's no time
for romance. Yet Giff seems to be in hot pursuit....
Is this part of his job, or can he really be falling
for her? And her chaotic, ready-made family!

**Available September 2010
wherever books are sold.**

"LOVE, HOME & HAPPINESS"